Two Supernatural Romance Novellas in One Volume!

The Amethyst Star

and

Creatures of the Night

by Karen Wiesner

Writers Exchange E-Publishing
http://www.writers-exchange.com/

The Amethyst Star

Futuristic Romance

They live in a time when humans have become an endangered species...

Thirty years ago, the men and women of Earth went off to fight in an intergalactic war. In the time since, carnivores have flourished and slaughtered most of the human race. Answering Earth's call for help to avoid extinction, Hunters have ultra-strength, speed and instincts, allowing them to destroy the carnivores. Human women have become invaluable prizes in their roles as Procreators. Pair-bonding is rare and families no longer exist. Lady Sher of the Amethyst Star is mankind's last hope for survival though her heart's desire can never be fulfilled...especially not with the hunter Randolf. On Randolf's home world, a vision of the rare star of amethyst was revealed along with the prophecy that if he loses this star, the hunter will become the hunted for all time. Will destiny and desire prove impossible goals?

Chapter 1

The Hunter raised his head in sudden awareness. Unlike the native inhabitants and even the chameleon Patrollers, who had also come to the Earth in the time of humankind's greatest need, Randolf and his Hunter brothers used the roadways of old instead of the rail conveyances that kept humans out of reach from the fortress walls and out of the sight and scent of the Carnivores.

All his senses attuned, Randolf turned slowly on the cracked tar, reached out to track with his keen sense of smell, his sensitive sight, his ultra-honed instincts. He probed beyond the steel fortress the humans had sealed themselves away inside from the thick jungle that had overrun the Earth in the time since the sun became one of their deadliest enemies. The Hunter and Patroller living areas, Comm Central, the City of Hope, and Castaway City—all lay within the fortress gates.

Darkness fell in a shroud across his path, and yet he could scent the tiger Carnivore, could feel its patient, mocking gaze despite the distance between them. This one wasn't like the ones he'd hunted and killed swiftly, with his bare hands and teeth. This one stalked him, eluded him. The vision...

Why do you watch me? Hunt me? Why do you not show yourself for what you are? You are not like the others.

Like a wind blowing through his mind, the words followed, not his own, and yet he knew they were truth. *I am not like the others. I am your destiny, Hunter. You will face me...and lose.*

Carnivores had no emotions and killed out of pure instinct, and yet they were clever. They had had no choice but to become so. Even before the men and women of Earth had fought in the first Intergalactic War thirty years earlier, their planet had begun turning on itself. The temperature had risen, increasing the carbon dioxide, and made prolonged exposure to the sun more deadly than ever before. Jungles and deserts had overtaken the Earth, and humans could survive only in jungle areas—the only place water and shelter remained. Unfortunately, Carnivores had risen to overtake the planet. Humankind—severely decreased in number—had returned to the Earth following the war to find their families slaughtered by the oversized man-eaters. In this time, men outnumbered women considerably.

Answering the humans' much belated cry for help, Hunters and Patrollers had come to the Earth and stopped the Carnivore blood baths. Humankind had sealed itself inside steel fortresses in an attempt to stop the Carnivores, yet despite the seemingly impenetrable fortress intended to keep them at bay, the beasts managed to kill even now. Always, they came without being seen, and though their coming was infrequent, they managed to kill stealthily and escape again unseen. The Hunters had searched endlessly and unsuccessfully without the fortress for the Carnivores' lair. It was as if the Carnivores had learned to control their hunger. No longer did they emerge and kill recklessly the way they had during the years war had taken most of the Earth's inhabitants and threatened those left behind to the point of near extinction. Perhaps, the Hunters had speculated, the Carnivores themselves were becoming extinct.

All along the road, Randolf stared through the closely-spaced, steel bars that rose nearly ten feet into the air and ended in sharp spikes, but the Carnivore had withdrawn. The jungle beyond the fortress enclosure felt silent and cloying, ripe with the scent of flowers, overgrown plants, and blood.

No, the blood was on him. Many a fortnight had passed since the Carnivores ventured inside the fortress walls. The humans were afraid and rarely ventured out into the open from their sealed homes and rail conveyances. This day, Randolf had tracked one with fierce hunger inside the gates. Tracked and killed it. But the man-eater had given him his scar. He looked down at the barely visible swipe of needle sharp claws that had raked his chest only once before he ripped its throat out with his teeth. Now he wore those very same claws around his neck as a souvenir of his victory this day. Tonight he and his brothers—the warrior priests from the planet Chaashane—would have fresh meat instead of the dried stores they had brought with them from their planet.

Turning aside, Randolf again moved in the direction of the Hunter Abode. Killing the Carnivores was his duty, and he had pledged his service to the wary humans for his four-year enlistment, which drew near its end. The needs of many outweighed the needs of one. Life must not be wasted. Humankind needed help if it were to survive the Carnivores and re-populate their planet again. All of their focus was on keeping their species alive and pure, so they accepted the help and protection given them by the Hunters and Patrollers. But they'd never liked them or welcomed them on their planet. Nevertheless, the Hunters considered it their duty to serve their Creator by serving all those who needed aid.

Nearly every human Randolf had met could be described in one word: Afraid. The humans were afraid of the Carnivores, afraid to hunt them by themselves, for fear of reducing their numbers again. Afraid of the toxic environment their own hands had brought about with their pollutants in the time past. Afraid of their protectors because of the special abilities they possessed and for the potential threat they posed in tainting the purity of their people. Most of all, they were afraid of dying out completely. Many of their warrior women who had fought in the Intergalactic War had rebelled against the decree of their elders passed long before the end of the war forbidding humans to pair-bond with other species.

The very few women on their planet—those who were capable of reproducing—were worshipped, coveted as their most valuable possessions, and given privileges no one was given on the planet. These women—Queens—had become nothing more than prized breeders. Once in a moon-cycle, their eggs were harvested in the attempt to "grow" a pure human race comparable to the days before their near extinction. The precious eggs were paired with sperm from only the strongest males and fertilized in a laboratory. Pair bonding was rare, allowed only in Castaway City, which was also within the enclosure, between sterile males and women who had failed to produce an heir. Families no longer existed in the City of

Hope since children were gestated in labs and raised in sex-specific institutions to eliminate the likelihood that humans would be exposed to alien races.

Nevertheless, in the thirty years since the war had ended, the human race had continued to die out. Randolf believed if they continued in their fearful, illogical ways, they would not pass another thirty years without becoming extinct. The elders had refused to listen to anyone's counsel save their own, shrugging off anything not resembling their 'scientific logic' as superstitious nonsense. Nevertheless, Randolf believed the Creator of the Universe had judged and passed sentence on their illogical need to control the uncontrollable, which had led them to futilely seek creation of pure humans untainted by the aliens in the universe around them.

Ahead, he could see the sprawling buildings of the Hunter Abode. As on their planet, all things connected, including family living spaces. The buildings on the Earth were not as elaborate as those on Chaashane, and the Hunters serving their tour of duty had brought very few possessions, as was their way. No home could equal the one on their own beloved planet. They accepted their role as protectors for a designated time—protectors with no mementos of home save those they wore on their person. The humans had given them a large parcel of land within the fortress walls far from their own dwellings, where Hunters and Patrollers took shifts around the clock guarding. Here in Hunter Abode, they could spend a few hours outside of the humans' unwelcoming tolerance. Or they had been able to until one Queen had done the unthinkable.

Randolf's far-seeing gaze sought and found the window within the Abode where he knew she would be standing. Lady Sher of the

Amethyst Star, a Queen and Procreator, had moved into the Hunter Abode two moon-cycles past. No one could have predicted it, could fathom it, nor could forbid it. As a Queen, all things were free to her on the planet. With her had come a garrison of Patrollers, further upsetting the balance of the Hunters' privacy and place of acceptance.

No one dared ask her *"Lady Sher, why have you come to live here among us?"* Randolf himself did not question her senseless decision. Because he knew.

Silhouetted in the growing darkness by the candlelight behind her, she stood in the window fragile and exquisite beyond anything he had ever seen. Without the light streaming in mercilessly during the day, she could tolerate this place she occupied when he came off-duty to his abode.

She risked the forbidden, unaware of her own intentions, he sensed. She, like the tiger carnivore that stalked him, was not like the others of her species. Unlike the rest of her people, Lady Sher of the Amethyst Star had absolutely no fear.

She had come to the Hunter Abode two moon-cycles previously to be nearer him just as he had taken a tour of duty to Earth to fulfill the vision foretold during his maturity ceremony. Randolf had come to meet his life-mate, sealed in the Amethyst Star.

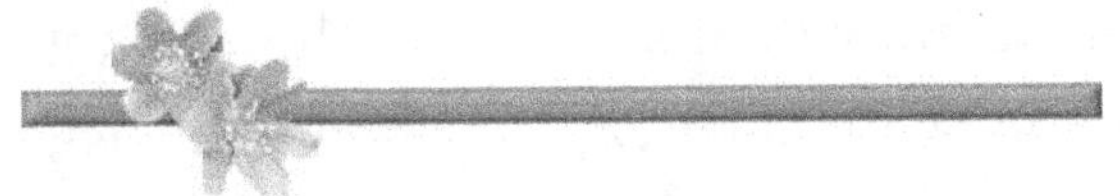

Sher didn't back away, out of the twilight, out of his reputedly sharp eyesight, even when Randolf looked up and searched out her window from more than a mile away.

How could she escape him? She had no desire to. For this very reason she'd come to the Hunter Abode. To watch him. To be near him. To fuel an obsession she knew could never be fulfilled the way she wished, was, in fact, forbidden by the laws of her people because she lived in a time when humans had become an endangered species.

Yet, as a Queen, she'd gone where previous procreators and those eventual ones wouldn't dare. What had she to fear, surrounded with protectors on the inside in the Patrollers, and protectors on the outside with the Hunters? Why shouldn't she know the state of their existence? Why shouldn't she live since she had no other hope in life?

After the age of sixteen, when she'd finally become a Queen, and the scientists could no longer forbid her, she'd spent much time listening to their advice. Finally, unable to keep herself from her own need for something more, she'd gone out of the palace, out of the City of Hope. Always surrounded by a garrison of the Patrollers—small, sleek, telepathic creatures that resembled the now extinct species of wolves she'd read about only in books; creatures that had a body chemistry that allowed them to surround anything and camouflage it so it appeared to disappear entirely—she had covered every inch inside the steel fortress. By day, she'd explored the communications center, which handled all intergalactic relations; the Headquarters for Safety and Regulations, where the Patrollers and Hunters checked in to their individual sections each day to give reports and receive orders; and even Castaway City, a place considered beneath a Queen.

Sher placed her fingertips against the glass as she recalled her travels and adventures, those few other Queens had experienced.

She'd also seen the Patrollers homes and social structures—strange, pod-like buildings that were made of a material unlike anything available on Earth, which they brought from their own planet. Earth was nearly as poisonous to the Patrollers as it had become to humans. Only by wearing special masks and inside their pods, which had the life-support suitable for them, could they survive for short amounts of time. They were a people who lived in a hive-mind structure that didn't encourage individualism. In appearance, each of them looked exactly the same without variation. With linked minds, they never acted as one, but as a group.

The Hunters were much different than the Patrollers—even in their living structures found only in Hunter Abode. Sher glanced around at the Hunter home she dwelled in. Their homes were no more than compartments where they slept, though all were linked together in a complex building. Socially, they gathered in a place within the building on the lower level that she'd heard called "The Tank", which was much like a dining room. There was a brotherhood between them. They each had personalities, and no two looked alike.

Randolf, in particular, intrigued her. Again, she glanced down from the window, searching out and finding him as he approached from the road. Unlike the other Hunters, who showed the proper deference to her by not meeting her gaze because of her status above all others on the planet, Randolf's eyes followed her whenever she went. She had never gone alone anywhere. The Patrollers went with her. And Randolf had been with her. He followed at a distance, yet she always felt him. Even when he was off-duty, he watched her.

Hunters had a very human appearance. However, their home-planet was very similar to current-day Earth, and they could tolerate the sun easily. Even among the various races still inhabiting the Earth, without the ability to be in the sun for long periods their skin had paled considerably. Hunters were all dark, with sharp, white teeth and pointed ears under the thick black hair that covered their heads. Thick eyebrows, the hair around their mouths and jaws, and their arms was also very dark and more abundant than on humans. She'd often wondered what their bodies were like beneath the sleeveless tunics, pants and boots they wore.

Randolf was nothing like the men, scientists and politicians, of Earth. His body moved like that of the Carnivores she foolishly wanted to see outside of books and old movies. Men on Earth, those who worked in the labs and institutions and congress, didn't look at women the way Randolf looked at her. In the quest to keep mankind pure, men and women were kept completely separate for most of their lives, except those males who served the females. Children and adults were also separated. No relationships, not even friendship, were ever forged between the sexes, or in units some might consider families. She would never know or recognize the children she produced for her people. The few times she'd asked after the eggs harvested from her, she'd been told it was not for her to know.

Things were different here in the Hunter Abode than the way they were in Castaway City. Life wasn't sterile, even within the enclosure as it was. Friendships were a strong part of their lives in this place. Humans had made them unwelcome despite their request for aid and the hesitant tolerance between Hunters and Patrollers, stemming from the Patrollers distrust given the fact that they couldn't sense Hunters the way they could every other species. Remaining with her hadn't been easy for them since she'd come here, but their sense of duty and obligation to her as a Queen prevented their departure.

She watched Randolf enter the designated city of his brother-warriors. No longer could she watch him from afar. As the only being capable of intimidating her, she relished a meeting between them. *"You must not go out, Lady Sher of the Amethyst Star,"* the Patroller hive insisted as one in her mind.

"It's evening. The sun won't harm me." Already, she moved toward the door.

"Carnivores prowl at night, Lady Sher of the Amethyst Star."

"You'll be there," she said confidently, and before her words had completed, they took up their places on all sides of her—not close enough to enact the invisible camouflage; nevertheless, ready at the slightest indication of danger to surround her.

Briskly, she moved down the stairs that led to the main level of the compound. As she did so, she lowered the gossamer veil over her face. The fabric was from another world, sheer and light, capable of protecting and providing her relief from head to toe against temporary exposure to the sunlight and the extreme humidity.

She emerged from the compound just as Randolf approached from the road. Though he didn't approach her as close as she would have liked and did lower his gaze and his head in deference, he took a risk no other would have. He met her eyes again as he said, *"Layus-mon* to you, milady" in the custom of his own people.

"Layus-mei, Hunter."

She saw his faint surprise and respect that she knew of his culture. More than any other people, she had studied those from the planet Chaashane.

"Carnivores hunt at night, Lady Sher. You are not safe outside at this time."

Only briefly, she glanced at the Patrollers around her. "As you can see, I'm well protected, Hunter."

The haughtiness in her own voice rang back at her, and she disliked it intensely. This was her first attempt to engage him in a conversation. Few would believe she lacked the courage to do so before now. She—the fearless Queen who'd broken all the unspoken rules by venturing outside the City of Hope, who had visited Comm Central, the off-worlders' headquarters and homes. She who had entered Castaway City, home to the scorned and forgotten. She who had made a home for herself where only Hunters inhabited. She who fulfilled her obligations to her people and who wanted to know the unknowable...with a Hunter.

Trying not to show her discomfort at his patience in waiting on her for either more conversation or dismissal, she said, "I so infrequently see the outside. Surely I'm allowed to when it's safe?"

"It's never safe, milady, but you have seen it all..." Once more, he lowered his gaze deferentially, but she sensed the amusement there, too. "As you say, Lady Sher. What have you to fear?"

Many considered her reckless. She was well aware that she was mankind's best hope. Previous Queens had been unable to reproduce for years and those offspring who had survived conception were rumored to have died at some point after their fifth year. No other females were of harvesting age aside from her. If she became lost or killed, the human race could become extinct. What right did she have to feel lonely? What right did she have to a personal life, aside from her role as little more than a breeder? What justification did she have for longing for an emotion long since banned for humans—for chosen ones? Her heart's desire could never be fulfilled, especially not with a Hunter, this very one who filled her every waking and dreaming mind with forbidden longings she couldn't begin to understand. What right did she have to want to understand these feelings inside her?

Around her, she sensed the unease of the Patrollers, yet this amused her because they usually lacked emotion. Standing with this Hunter had them on edge, and, as her gaze met Randolf's dark, compelling one, she realized that he shared her amusement about this.

"Perhaps you'd like to stay and ascertain my safety as well, Hunter?" she said softly, unwilling to let her glance stray from his.

He didn't disappoint her when he matched her unwillingness to stray from their meeting. "If you wish, Lady Sher, I am at your disposal."

Warmth she couldn't name filled her face. Technically, he was off-duty for the night, and she'd seen the importance the Hunters placed on joining together, talking, connecting with one another. Yet she couldn't help her nod as she glanced around at the compound, where Hunters watched them without direct interest.

Life was so different here than in the City of Hope. Her people were focused entirely on procreation, reproduction, avoiding extinction at all cost. All study was based in some part on learning the past, present, and future of the human race so the scientists and politicians could debate how best to act now to achieve the desired result of repopulating the Earth with humans. But here life buzzed with colors and scents, things to do and listen to. They laughed in this place, something she'd never heard until she ventured out of the city of the chosen. Hunters played and listened to music as entertainment instead of purely for education. They played games outside of those that enriched the mind. No, life here wasn't sterile. It was primal, and, since she'd come here to live, she'd felt a kind of excitement she couldn't explain.

Conversations within the City of Hope amounted to question and answer exchanges, commands, and those debates and lectures associated with politics and education. Now that she'd secured a legitimate reason for Randolf to stay with her, her mind became a blank. He continued to watch her in an intense way that would have been reprimanded anywhere outside of the Hunter Abode. His gaze seemed to see right through her, and she couldn't help noticing the way his eyes drifted over her body before returning to her face. The warmth in her face increased, and she took an uncontrollable step toward him. The scent of him so close made the blood race wildly in her veins.

"Your day of hunting was a success?" she asked, seeing the necklace of Carnivore claws that signaled a kill to his people. He would be honored this night with his people...once she allowed him to leave her side. She knew his kill had been logged at the S&R headquarters and then delivered to their city for consumption. She also knew she should have been disgusted by it and the scent of the cooking meat that permeated the whole of the city. Her people were brought up to abhor meat and killing, but she couldn't help her fascination with their customs.

"Yes," Randolf responded. "Today, I have had success. Perhaps you would care to join my brothers and I for the celebratory dinner?"

His invitation shocked her, and she spluttered in protest, "But...you...you eat the meat of your kill, Hunter!"

Smiling slightly, he nodded. "That I do, milady. Very few races who do not are as strong as we are. In this way, we honor the life taken because we waste nothing."

Sher turned away, wanting to deny the weakness of her own species. As they could no longer tolerate their own climate or the now dominant species on the planet, her people had become vegetarians, subsisting on the plants they grew within the fortress. Though many claimed it was a choice made to strengthen their people, logic told her they'd had *little* choice in the matter. And the smell of the roasting meat, far from disgusting, forced her to admit to herself that, given the choice again, most humans would be carnivores themselves. Her own meal of vegetables and fruits had done nothing to calm the raging hunger the scent coming through her window tonight had caused.

The Patrollers surrounding her suddenly became wary, and she pivoted her glance around her to find Randolf so close to her, her breath suspended in her throat.

"Is that a refusal to my invitation, Lady Sher?"

She saw his teeth—blindingly white, and sharp as daggers—and his firm, soft lips curled around them, and her heart thrilled within her. He wasn't human, despite a resemblance to humans. Humans must never pair bond with any other race. It was their law. Yet she would have liked nothing better than to touch her own mouth to his.

What did she know of being social, of interacting with a man? She knew nothing. Only that this hunter had filled her every thought since the very first time she saw him. Her unexplainable longings, her loneliness, had grown out of the very need she had to be near him. Next to him. Close enough to touch him and never stop. She wanted the forbidden. The one thing she could never have.

Just as sudden as the Patrollers' wariness came Randolf's own. He crouched, eyes narrowing to slits, teeth bared, nose working the air. Without looking at her, he urged her back toward the compound. "You must go inside, milady. It is not safe here."

A second later, he bounded away with the other Hunters in a blur of speed and strength, affecting her as much as his nearness had. But, when the Patrollers surrounded and whisked her back inside, she couldn't murmur the slightest protest.

Chapter 2

No, this Carnivore was like no other. He had followed Randolf to the Hunter village this night, risking its life to come to the place of their only real threat on the planet. Randolf could not understand this course of action. He had felt this particular Carnivore before, though much more of late. At first, he had assumed it stalked him.

This night, Randolf had to ask himself whether it was a coincidence that the Carnivore had been coming oft since Lady Sher had moved into the Hunter Abode. Was this unique man-eater after him? Or Lady Sher of the Amethyst Star?

Though reason said she was safest in this place than anywhere else on Earth, Randolf now faced the strong possibility that the Hunter Abode had become too dangerous for her to continue here. For that reason alone, he risked another foolish conversation with her. The time of his awareness to his life-mate was coming upon him, and the more he saw her, the longer he dwelled in her very presence, the more helpless he became to his own feelings and desires for her.

His brother Hunters did not understand why she had come to their village. Nevertheless, each of them knew what his maturity ceremony vision had dictated. In the traditional Chaashane ceremony that came to all males of their race at the age of seventeen, Randolf and his clan priest had shared a vision of his life-mate. Both saw the rare star of amethyst. When the call for Hunters to go to Earth for service had come and he had seen Lady Sher of the Amethyst Star himself, his destiny led him forward. He had come to Earth to find his life-mate, but he had realized in little time that his vision could not be. Humans were forbidden to pair bond with any other race.

His brother Hunters and her own people could not understand how drawn she was to him. Her life consisted of little more than being a breeder. From the time she was old enough to understand, she had been told exactly what would be expected of her as a female. And she had been accorded all the honor of her role as Queen. Her people could forbid nothing of her, yet, despite her search for it, she had no freedom. The boundary of her obligations to the entire human race had been clearly marked. She pushed the limits but never crossed them. Randolf understood that she wanted a semblance of a life of her own. What was she willing to do to get it, though? What could he allow?

Taking the stairs to her rooms in the compound, he felt the lack of ease in the Patrollers long before he knocked on her door and she opened to him. He could see her surprise in the widening of her eyes, the sudden color in her alabaster face. Uncontrollably, his gaze traveled hungrily over the thin garb she wore to protect herself from the sun. The sheer fabric performed the very task required yet hid little of the sensual curves it draped. He could easily trace the shape of her breasts with his gaze, the taut lines of her long legs and gently rounded hips.

Chaashane women were dark, muscular, and primal even as they were reverent of propriety. Light even at her white-blond hair—where the thin, silver crown she wore insetted with the Star of Amethyst rested atop—Lady Sher was soft, willowy, and seemed to float in the delicate way her pet butterflies did when she moved. She understood nothing of propriety, for she had no idea the pleasures the men and women even in her own human past and those of other species could enjoy together. Yet he sensed she wanted him as he wanted her.

Randolf forced himself to look away from her at the few rooms that she'd decorated with the brightest of jewel colors. Inside a huge glass bottle the shape of a teardrop, yellow, gold, blue, black, and multi-colored butterflies flitted. The bottle had been filled with plants and flowers to provide oxygen.

"Is there a Carnivore in the village?" she asked softly, and he could not resist the lure of her voice. Facing her again, he looked into the almond shaped eyes the color of lavender, so like the amethysts that were the rarest jewel in the universe. The only planet that retained a few of the gems was Earth.

"It has disappeared, milady, but you are not safe here. I believe this Carnivore is stalking you."

No surprise lighted her eyes. "But all Carnivores stalk humans. It's their way."

"You misunderstand me, Lady Sher. This Carnivore stalks you in particular."

"Because I'm away from the City of Hope," she said on a shrug, turning and draping herself over a couch. Her garrison of Patrollers allowed her more distance they then would have outside of her rooms. "Surely this is the safest place I can be. But, in truth, where is safe for humans?"

"You are of great value to your people, milady—you above all others."

"I assure you, I realize that, Hunter," she said in the cold way she did to everyone but him. "Do you think I'm not aware of my value every second of every minute of every hour of every day of my life?"

"As you say, Lady Sher," he murmured deferentially and felt her gaze turn back to him.

"Do you understand, Randolf?"

"Yes."

He could not keep himself apart from her. The need to get closer overtook him. More than anything, he wanted to allow himself to see the satin sheen of her skin, to smell the scent of flowers all around her and the musk her own body produced especially now. The time of her ovulation was near. And his awareness pierced him sharply as his body reacted violently to her nearness. The very hair on his arms stood on end as hot blood coursed through him.

"I understand, milady, but you would be safer inside the City of Hope." *There, I can at least protect you from my own needs, needs that would break your laws.*

"How?" she asked harshly, and he heard tears behind her words, tears that sparkled in her eyes as well. "How can I be safe there? I can't live there anymore. I can't *breathe* there. There is no freedom in those gates. I'm not free anywhere I go, but I want something. Something for myself. How can you understand that, Hunter?"

"Because I am free. You have made no choices, milady. You are bound by the very role that gives you honor. I am a priest of my people, a prince, yet I choose. I could not live the way you have no choice but to live."

A silver tear ran down her cheek, and Randolf kneeled before her to catch it in his palm. She glanced down as he opened his moist hand. The blaze of amethyst from the oval jewel in her crown caught the candlelight and lavender blazed against the single teardrop.

"I'm not free. I know nothing of love," she whispered. "I know only of duty, and I know I must not jeopardize my people. I'll fulfill my obligations. I'll do it from here as long as I will."

"As you say, Lady Sher."

Lifting his hand, he kissed his own palm, then stood and left her rooms, drawing in the gasp she uttered as if it could sustain his awareness. Yet the weight of the amulet he wore about his neck, beneath his tunic, felt heavier than ever before. Randolf reached for it, the star of amethyst forged after the shared vision of his life-mate. He pressed the oval jewel against his palm and felt seared with his own needs.

So it began. The time of his awareness would henceforth become uncontrollable, and unbearable, until his life-mate either became his for eternity or the prophecy of loss that completed his maturity ceremony came true.

She could feel that kiss against his palm as if he'd kissed her. Sher closed her eyes to sleep, but that kiss seared through her mind until her every sense came down to him.

For hours after Randolf's departure from her rooms, she'd heard the celebration in his honor and wanting to be with him was unbearable.

Why had he come to her? Did he really want her to leave, or was he just being protective? His race was known for their unselfishness. She could believe he felt an obligation, similar to her own, to see to it that he protected humankind, especially the Queens.

"As you say, Lady Sher." Lifting his hand, he kissed his palm, the palm he'd caught her tear in.

Sher closed her eyes tightly, wanting to sob her frustration.

Why does search me out? Why does he follow me everywhere I go? Why does he look at me the way he does? Hungrily. As if...as if he wants to touch me the way I've only dreamed of touching him.

She wouldn't take lightly the warning that the Carnivore stalked her personally. The thought terrified her. She'd never seen a Carnivore, though she'd almost been attacked twice. The Patrollers and Hunters had rescued her long before the man-eater got close enough to her for her to see it. Leaving the palace after both episodes had been difficult, but she refused to live her life in fear. She was a prisoner, a glorified breeder, but she wouldn't be afraid.

Carnivores were said to be stealthy and clever, entering any place unseen, attacking swiftly, and departing unseen as well. But an attack was distinctive. Rarely did they leave much behind outside of a trail of blood from the victim. Attacks had become infrequent in the years since the Patrollers and Hunters heeded the call for aid, but the Carnivores always came sooner or later, when their hunger drove them to desperation. Why would any of the Carnivores target her specifically? They couldn't distinguish between male and female; to them, she was little more than meat. Or did they understand that females were the last hope of the human race? How could they? Yet Randolf had said this Carnivore was stalking her in particular.

She rose from her bed, the Patrollers instantly surrounding her. Sighing, she walked through them to the window and looked down at the grounds. From her window, she saw a figure on the bottom of the staircase leading to her rooms.

Randolf. He watched over her, even here.

As if he sensed her, he turned and their eyes met. The look in his made her catch her breath. In the distance between them, they touched in a way they hadn't dared to previously and the intimacy made her feel ravenous for more.

In another time, another place, I would belong to you, Hunter. And you would belong to me. But what can we have together now, in this time, in this place? What is allowed of even a Queen, the last hope of her people? What consolation if the answer is nothing?

Chapter 3

"You have had no sleep this night, brother Amethyst," Hunter Bodie said, teasing with the name Randolf had been dubbed by the population after his shared vision as he patrolled the village a third time that evening. "Lady Sher is well protected here."

Was she? Randolf was no longer as sure. How were the Carnivores entering the steel gates? Their entrance and exit had still not been discovered in the two decades since the Hunters came to Earth. Every possibility of a breach had been gone over time and time again. Even in the last few years, three precious humans had been attacked and taken. And if Lady Sher was being stalked personally by this unique man-eater, Randolf would not sleep to keep her safe.

"I find myself unable to be far from her."

Bodie nodded. "As you say, brother. You have not been far from her since she re-located to our village and you requested Hunter perimeter security, behind the Patrollers."

Randolf closed his hand, fisted it, still feeling the teardrop inside his palm. Her world was not something he could understand. He respected it, yet he found it unfathomable for a culture to survive without family. Without love. Without pair bonding. Without reverence for how the Creator intended life to be. Above all else, Randolf's people valued family and mates. Save for worship and service to the Creator of the Universe, nothing else held more value on Chaashane. And Lady Sher would never have that.

Oh, he had heard the human scientists and politicians debating endlessly the proper course of action, the course that would ensure survival and purity of the human race. Namely, keeping themselves separate from other species by outlawing pair bonding with others, outlawing the possibility of "half-breed" children that would dilute the human race until it no longer existed in its purest form. Yet, even among their own kind, they refused to pair-bond, believing it would limit the number of humans they could "grow" if women weren't used as breeders and their eggs weren't harvested and fertilized in droves during every moon-cycle. The humans had enough eggs to re-populate the Earth three times over, from previous breeder Queens. Randolf had heard the rumors that the humans hadn't produced an heir that lived past the age of five in many years.

Had they even fertilized any of Lady Sher's eggs? What must it be like for her to know her eggs were to be fertilized and the offspring raised without love in a laboratory instead of in her home, with her and her life-mate? What must it be like for her to know she would never meet, nor rear, any of her own children? He could only guess at her loneliness because of what he felt for his family back on Chaashane, but hers was an eternal loneliness.

Bodie sat with him on the stair, a worried expression on his face. "You are not yet twenty-one years, my brother. You have not reached the age of awareness to your life-mate. Has something happened?"

Chaashane people reached awareness at the age of twenty-one and only after they had met their life-mate. At that time, the sexual drive became active and intolerable. On his home world, all inhabitants mated for life. Without Sher...

"I feel her, I sense her without ceasing."

"Then it has begun," Bodie said heavily. "She is a human Queen. It is illegal for her to take a life-mate, whether human or otherwise. And they fear us despite their need of us."

"Yes," Randolf agreed.

"Your shared vision is impossible, brother Amethyst."

"Yes."

Bodie did not give voice to the other truth they both knew. If the shared vision was impossible, that left the prophecy—the third part of the maturity ceremony—as the only possible outcome.

As soon as she saw Randolf coming home the next evening, Sher sent one of her Patrollers down—against its will—to him. After a day of wondering how she could find a way to see him and talk to him again, this was the only way.

From her window, she saw her Patroller returning, and her chest felt tight enough to explode as she waited for word. Obviously not happy, the Patroller said in her mind simply, *"He accepts, Lady Sher of the Amethyst Star. He will call for you shortly."*

Waiting the five minutes Randolf required was beyond her bearing. She felt breathless when she opened the door at his knock.

"*Layus-mon,* Lady Sher," he said with a nod that didn't satisfy her in the least.

"*Layus-mei,* Randolf. I'm still welcome to join you for dinner this night?"

"As you say, milady. Most welcome."

She swallowed the lump that had formed in her throat at the sight of him, and, at his encouragement, preceded him down the staircase with her entourage of bodyguards to The Tank. Even from afar, she could smell the ripe, succulent scents of roasting meat, so unlike the fruits and vegetables she'd eaten all her life, and the ale Hunters preferred and brought with them from their planet.

Randolf opened the door for her, and she saw inside that the dining room was filled with the fragrant candles she'd come to prefer to the artificial lights of the City of Hope. She felt no surprise at the abrupt silence that filled the huge room. Everywhere she went, she surprised those there with her unexpected presence. She greeted them with a haughty nod that reminded them silently that she was a Queen and free to move about as she pleased.

Behind her, Randolf pointed to an empty table and she walked to it. He eased the chair out for her and waited for her to be seated and to invite him to join her before he sat across from her. The Patrollers clearly didn't approve and finally settled near the front door.

She glanced around at the room filled with intricately carved furniture made of a type of wood native to Chaashane.

"We offer only Hunter fare here, milady. Does the scent of

roasting meat disgust you?"

She had no reason to uphold human customs, especially this one. Eating meat wasn't against the law. It was simply tradition.

"On the contrary, Hunter, it tantalizes me."

"Is it not forbidden, Lady Sher?" That not quite smile hovered under the surface of his hard, beautiful face.

She quite believed this Hunter knew far more about humans than they did of him and his people. "Nothing is forbidden for a Procreator," she said simply.

He nodded. "As you say."

With that, he made a motion that she realized was an order to bring food and drink. A moment later, one of the Hunters brought them a tray with a loaf of dark bread, seared, pinkish mounds she knew had to be meat, and large tankards of an amber liquid.

Sher glanced around, listening for a moment to the renewed foreign speech around them.

"Are you a warrior even on your own planet, Randolf? Is Randolf really your name?" she asked, trying not to show as much interest as she felt in the slicing of the bread and the fragrant meat that made her mouth water.

"Randolf is as close to my real name as humans can pronounce. I am a prince, milady. My clan is the oldest, and we are priests of the highest order of the Creator of the Universe. We serve our Creator by serving all those who need aid."

She'd heard that the Hunters were an unselfish people. This proved it. "Who is in your clan?" she asked just as the Hunter set a wooden plate with bread and meat on it before her. After setting one also before Randolf, the Hunter nodded deferentially to both of them, then left them alone.

Randolf seemed to sense that she didn't know what to do with the unfamiliar food. He lifted the meat in his hand, tore off a chunk of it with his teeth, and she stifled the gasp of shocked pleasure she felt as he swallowed. "My clan is made up of many generations," he said after a moment. "Chaashane inhabitants live very long lives and we produce plentifully in a short time. Eighteen generations live within the Chaashane abode."

"Children live with you?" she asked, tentatively lifting the meat in her fingers.

"Of course. Individual family units, as well as the clan, help to raise our young."

She brought the meat to her lips, and did as Randolf did, tearing a small bit of it off with her teeth. The meat was tender enough to melt in her mouth, bursting flavor unlike anything she'd ever tasted through her senses as she chewed it. She enjoyed the texture far more than she'd expected to. "I have no family," she murmured. "I always knew what my life would be."

"It is not good to be alone."

"Are you alone?" she asked after she'd eaten another, larger, bite of the meat. "On your home world?"

"All Chaashane inhabitants mate for life. We do not reach the age of awareness until we have passed twenty-one years."

"How old are you?"

"I will be twenty-one in one moon-cycle."

"I can't imagine," she murmured. "I can't understand."

She watched him eat the bread and reached for her own. The nutty flavor enhanced the meat and the smooth amber liquid.

"Hunters respect all customs. But those of your race, milady, we do not understand." His black eyes seemed to penetrate straight into the feelings she'd never shared with anyone before.

"We do what we have to do to survive," she insisted.

"Do you?" he asked, and she sensed though didn't hear doubt in his tone.

"What do you mean, Hunter?"

"I speak too freely, milady." He lowered his eyes deferentially.

She shook her head. "No, I want to know what you meant by that. Our scientists have studied all ways and all cultures and customs since before the Intergalactic War ended and some returned to a decimated planet. They've determined that the human race can only survive as we do now—without intermingling with other species and without pair bonding. If we pair bonded, only one egg at a time could be fertilized. Twins, triplets...these things are unheard of for humans."

"This has not always been so, milady. And in the thirty years since the end of the war, your population is no greater than it was when your warriors returned."

He didn't say what he could have. The population was only *half* of what it'd been even then.

"Not for lack of trying," she murmured.

"As you say, Lady Sher."

He accepted what she said, she sensed, but he didn't agree with it. She'd known very little outside of her own culture. Yet the memory of what she'd accidentally stumbled upon in Castaway City... She vividly recalled the man and woman who came together in a stolen tryst behind the social building. They'd whispered of love. Of permanency. Their mouths had touched, opened to one another. Hands had moved freely over nudity, lips trailing after. And the joining, the things they had done together, and Sher had witnessed from a hiding place, had brought them such pleasure, they'd cried out as they clung together in earnest, as if they would fly apart without that protective hold of each other.

She'd never gone back to Castaway City. Nor had she been able to erase the sensual, exciting images from her mind. Whenever her mind fell into the dream-state, she imagined Randolf the Hunter's mouth on hers, her own opening beneath his. She imagined his hands and his mouth exploring her body freely.

"What do you say?" she asked Randolf. "Why do you think we humans have been unable to reproduce and re-populate these many years?"

"Who can be certain?"

"But what do you think?"

"At your request, milady, the only logical answer is that pair bonding is the will of the Creator of the Universe. Children were not meant to be born in a lab and reared without families. The problems that your planet faces are in direct relationship to your elders' need to control what should only be controlled by the Creator."

"I was born and raised in a lab," she insisted, but was reminded by her own mind that she was one of the last to have done so. A successful birth and raising past five years of age hadn't been achieved in many years, according to the rumors the elders refused to confirm.

"As you say. But it is not meant to be."

"But how would we re-populate the Earth with so few women to pair-bond with? So many eggs would go to waste each month!"

"How did your world begin? Your own texts point to one man and one woman from whom your world became filled to over-abundance. Your forsaken and banished have already discovered the truth. The Earth belongs to the Creator and His ways." He'd cleared his plate and glanced up at her. "And yet your scientists and politicians debate endlessly about matters that are obvious to everyone else. This problem your planet faces is not one that can be solved by science, but by a spiritual reawakening."

She'd never considered it in this way before. Adam and Eve, the first man and woman, were spoken of in some of their most ancient books—books the elders rejected as mere fairy tales. Could the Earth be filled again by a new Adam and Eve? It was unthinkable. The human elders would never consider it. Since before the Intergalactic War, they had tried to solve all problems the planet faced scientifically, logically, they assumed.

"I saw no children in Castaway City. I saw only castaways and Hunters," she insisted.

"Because you did not visit the outcasts' homes during the day. Your visit was at night, and only in the social places."

How could it be? And yet Randolf could go anywhere within the fortress walls by day. Who would know better?

"How is it the elders don't know this, Hunter?" she asked.

"Who has returned to the City of Hope once banished? And who within the City of Hope would visit Castaway City if not banished there?"

Stunned, she shook her head. "Hunters go there."

"Yes. Some of my people live there, milady."

"Live?"

"Some have taken life-mates with the castaways of your people."

Her mind couldn't conceive of what he told her so plainly. Children? Castaways had children together? Conceived children with Hunters? "How many?" she asked in barely a whisper.

"The city overflows with them, milady. Boys and girls."

"The elders must know! They must be told!"

"Your elders, Lady Sher, refuse to believe the truth, certainly not enough to go there and see it. And they would refuse to accept 'half-breeds' into the pure line they hold dearly to, would they not?"

Her first thought was that she must go there herself, to verify it, but she knew she didn't need to go herself. She knew Randolf spoke the truth. The castaways, who no longer had any obligation to their own people, were breeding—naturally. They were mingling with Hunters and reproducing. But would the elders refuse to accept them as the true last hope for mankind?

"Come, milady. The hour grows late," Randolf said when she'd finished everything on her plate.

She nodded, uncertain what to do now. Her meals had always been left and cleaned up by a palace servant inside the City of Hope. She had served herself here of what she'd brought along. Randolf thanked his brothers, helped her rise from her chair, then she preceded him out of The Tank. Her protectors moved into a loose formation around her and Randolf.

"Your people will hear of what you have done this night," Randolf said in a low voice as they crossed the grounds.

Sher deliberately slowed her step. "I'm certain they won't understand this any more than they understand anything I do."

When she glanced at him, she saw an approving smile on his irresistible mouth. How could she let this moment pass? "I wish you to accompany me to my rooms," she said softly.

Randolf halted, and she faced him. "I'm certain that is not wise, milady."

"Nevertheless…"

"It is not proper, Lady Sher."

"There remains a fragment of light," she said.

He nodded, but his eyes never left hers. "As you say, milady."

She swallowed the lump in her throat, forced herself to turn and walk away, leaving him with her haughty expectations, "Then I shall await you at deep nightfall, Hunter."

Chapter 4

Several brother hunters came to Randolf after he saw Lady Sher enter her rooms in safety.

"This is a dangerous game you play, Randolf of Amethyst. This Queen is no castaway. She is forbidden to you. The humans are watching the two of you. If they believe Lady Sher grows too close to you, my brother, they will bring her back to the palace and refuse to allow her outside the city again."

"She is my destiny." And he well knew their bond had already gone too far to pull back now. Not without taking the risk of losing her for all time. His need to belong to her, to take and give love with her as his life-mate, had become almost more than he could bear.

"Perhaps it would have been better had you not taken your tour of duty, brother," Bodie suggested gently.

Perhaps, but he had had no choice but to come. None of them would have turned away from their destiny either. It was simply too strong to fight.

A maturity ceremony consisted of three parts and each bound the seeker to his or her destiny for all time. First, the clan priest and the seeker shared a vision. Both Randolf and his priest had seen clearly the rare star of amethyst. Next, the clan priest forged the amulet that sealed the vision. The amethyst star within Randolf's amulet had been extremely difficult to come by and had required sacrifices from himself and his family to procure. Without foreseeing Lady Sher himself, the clan priest had forged the amulet exactly like the one in Lady Sher of the Amethyst Star's crown. The very instant Randolf had heard the call for Hunters to go to Earth and serve the Queen Lady Sher, he had known and accepted that destiny called him. Finally, to counterbalance the vision of life, the clan priest gave the prophecy of loss: If Randolf lost the star of amethyst, the hunter would become the hunted for all time.

Prophecies were never fully understood until the time was full for their meaning to become clear. Randolf understood already that there was a strong risk that he would lose the star of amethyst. Humans had outlawed pair bonding with any other race. Destiny and desire proved impossible to fulfill. Yet he knew he must be with her. He must give everything to gain life and his eternity with his forechosen life-mate. Where once he could stay in the shadows to watch over and protect her, now his awareness had grown too strong because of her proximity. He had no control over his needs.

At once dark nightfall came, he was outside her door, and in a moment she opened to him and drew him inside. He sensed the Patrollers, but, no doubt on her command, they were deeper in the rooms, away from them.

"Tell me your heart, milady," he said softly, holding her so fiercely, he feared he would bruise her. She did not draw away from him, but returned his hold.

"I don't know it," she answered, and he sensed her innocence in these matters. "I know I saw them together, the man and woman in Castaway City…" She drew back only enough to gaze upon his face. "I saw this touching, holding each other, their mouths as one, their bodies…joined. I felt their desire, their love, and I knew."

"What did you know, Lady Sher?"

"That I must be with you that same way, even if it's forbidden."

The agony he felt tore at him like a living thing, hunting him, teasing him, refusing to release him. Or her.

"If ever I hold you in that way, milady, more so than this, I cannot promise you I can draw back."

Her eyes shone like jewels in the candlelight, her face smooth, perfect alabaster. Randolf helplessly traced the fullness of her lips, experiencing their moisture when she kissed his fingers.

"You are forbidden to me, milady. By your own laws. And yet I would have you for my own for all time. I hold a prophecy of loss, but what is yours, Lady Sher? What risks do you take that you will accept without regret? I would rather have nothing than your regret."

She closed her eyes, leaning toward him, nuzzling him. The butterfly brush of her satin mouth against his skin undid him. He stroked her face, her lips again, hot blood surging like lava through his body.

"If your elders take you from here, if they forbid you to return, to see me, will you regret then, milady? Tell me your heart in this before I cannot turn back!"

Her eyes opened, heavy with desire as her fingertips stroked his jaw, his chin, his own mouth. He could not wait for a moment longer for her reply. Lifting her face, he brought his lips to her own, swift and sure.

In that instant, their pair bond was complete. She belonged to him. He belonged to her. A union blessed by the Creator of the Universe. Her body molded itself to his, and she sighed. Her long fingers delved into his hair and danced at the pointed tips of his ears. Even amidst the scents of the many candles burning, her femininity filled his nostrils. But what of tomorrow? Would there be a tomorrow for them? And, in that tomorrow, would she regret giving herself to him? Would he lose her forever, giving ground to the prophecy of loss? All of her life, she had been told that she was the last hope of her people.

"Milady," he whispered, drawing his mouth to her ear. She grabbed hold of him tightly. "This very night, I would impregnate you. Maybe not the first time, but soon after. That is certain if you allow it."

He eased back and saw the wideness of her eyes. She had been thinking only of the vision she had seen of love between the human male and female, never considering that that love could create a life within her—one that was not allowed by the elders.

"How do you know...? How can you be sure...?" she began helplessly.

"That I would impregnate you, milady? Chaashane men can sense much more than human males, and we are designed for reproduction and raising families. Fertilization will take place during the first or second coupling without a doubt. And the child will be born in only five moon-cycle's time."

Surprising him, she took a step backward, her expression drawn and confused. Her innocence had not allowed her to consider past a stolen moment together. She had not considered consequences. The very real consequence of facing the elders, being made to feel that she was letting down her people by selfishly taking what she wanted.

"You should not have the fate of your people resting on your shoulders, Lady Sher. If you are not free, then what is life? Why is life worth fighting for without freedom?"

But he could see that having the fate of her people resting on her shoulders was a burden she had accepted from the start. She would not easily throw it off her.

"I'm free, but they need me," she said with much uncertainty.

Randolf did not argue. Her choice was her own. "As you say, milady."

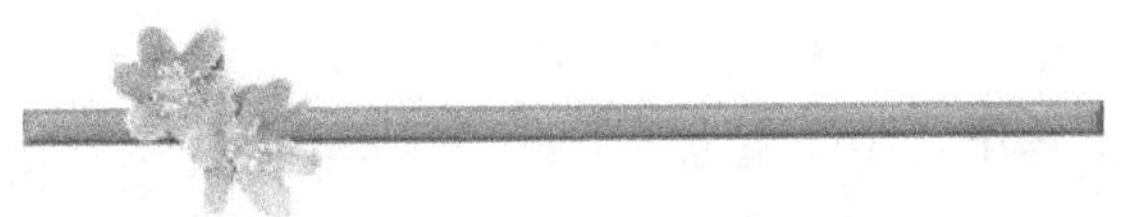

Though she'd hoped no word had gotten out of her previous night's activities, Sher wasn't surprised when Patrollers knocked on her door the next morning to inform her that a conveyance had been sent to summon her to the City of Hope. Refusal would have implied more than she was willing to risk. Yet her worry when she was safely on the windowless, cool train and railing back to the palace overwhelmed her. This was certainly different than all the times she'd previously gone out and done things the elders would disapprove of on principle.

How much did they know? That she'd eaten meat? That she'd eaten it with the Hunter Randolf? That she'd kissed him and considered much more than that before she'd heard that pregnancy…not a sterile, laboratory pregnancy…would result.

Who did she belong to? Herself? Her people? What was freedom? She'd been told all her life that she was free, but she knew deep down it wasn't true. How could she be free? She had an obligation to her people and the elders would never allow her to forget it. In truth of fact, they allowed her to roam where she liked, even lived where she liked. She knew if she ever did anything that went against the dictates they'd set down after the first Intergalactic war, she would be forbidden to leave the palace. She would be a prisoner there, never to roam outside, never to see Randolf again.

Without a life or choices, she had no life. Yet her choices could decide the fate of her people.

Immediately after disembarking from the rail train, she was led to the laboratory, where the machines there poked and prodded her for many hours. For the first time, as she lay in the cold, white room, she realized how much she dreaded coming to this room. The processing of having her eggs harvested by a machine was…invasive, and she suffered many days afterward with cramps and bleeding. Sometimes she could hardly walk.

But this day, she wouldn't have to undergo the harvesting. She wasn't sure what they were looking for until the robotic, disembodied voice of which she'd been told all her life belonged "to the elders" came into her silent, lonely palace apartments hours later.

"The time of your next ovulation is very near, Lady Sher."

"Yes."

"You would do well to remain in the palace, as you'll be ready for harvesting in four days' time," the voice told her.

Sher was aware that she was being watched, and, as with the Patrollers, this had never bothered her before, until today. What freedom if she never had any privacy?

"You were seen the night previously in the Hunter social building. It is rumored you ate meat."

"Is that why you spent so many hours poking and prodding me today?" she asked before she could think better of it.

A long pause followed, and her own anger at their audacity surprised her. "Humans ate meat for centuries before the dark days," she said firmly. "Those in Castaway City also eat meat shared with them by the Hunters."

"Such practices do not befit a Queen of your stature. Nor does spending time associating with a Hunter, particularly that same Hunter who entered your rooms after dark." The voice—previously unemotional—became decidedly impatient.

The Patrollers reported hourly to the elders. Their loyalty to her extended only in the form of protection.

Sher clasped her hands together as she sat on the sofa fighting her frustration. "The logic of begging off-worlders to aid us in our fight against the Carnivores only to treat them like unwanted intruders is lost on me," she said clearly. But she understood the elders' fears. Friendship with off-worlders could lead to pair bonding and illegal intermingling of humans and other species. What would they do if they knew that the castaway humans were pair bonding with Hunters and with each other and producing children in great numbers naturally, with no science involved?

For a moment, she considered telling them, but as Randolf had said—they wouldn't believe it. Nor would they do anything to verify the fact.

"You are a Queen, Lady Sher, and your responsibility is to the purity and reproduction of your people."

And if she failed in either of those respects...she would bear the full weight of her failure. She would be banished from the City of Hope and forgotten. In some ways, she envied the men and women of Castaway City. Yes, they were scorned, considered failures to the human race, but they were also free to find love, to live life without any boundaries or obligations. They were free to choose their own destiny. Maybe their curse was a blessing after all.

"I'm returning to Hunter Abode today," Sher decided suddenly, standing. The Patrollers immediately surrounded her.

"Lady Sher, that isn't possible. You will be ready for harvest in just..."

"I will return in three days' time."

She didn't wait for a refusal or protest. Half expecting to be detained, she walked briskly to the conveyance, thinking of only one thing.

Freedom.

Chapter 5

Randolf could see the heaviness of the Queen's heart as he followed her as closely as he dared throughout the day. His presence was never questioned, nor did Lady Sher seem aware of his presence so wrapped up in her thoughts was she. Until he saw her emerge from the palace and quickly enter the conveyance, he believed with anguish that he might never see her again.

When her train arrived in Hunter Abode, he rushed ahead and waited on the platform for her. His heart thrilled at the light in her eyes at the sight of him.

"You were summoned, milady?" he asked without preface, a little desperately.

"Yes."

"Questioned about your activities, but allowed to go at your wish?"

She took a deep, uncertain breath. "Yes."

While she did not speak of it, he knew as well as she did that, should she be summoned again, she would not be allowed to leave the palace.

"Why did you leave the City of Hope, Lady Sher? Why did you return to this place?"

She looked at him, and her feelings for him were tender to the very depths of her gaze. "I want freedom, Hunter, with you. But you'll be banished from Earth if you make the same choice I have."

When they reached the door of her rooms, she turned back to the Patrollers. "I wish to be alone. You may wait below on the stair landing."

The united protest Randolf knew came from the chameleons was lost on her. She closed the door after the two of them entered and immediately slid into his arms. The feel and scent of her filled him with an unspeakable longing that he knew would not be controlled this night.

"Tell me why you're here with me, Randolf," she asked, her eyes locked with his.

"You are my vision, my rare star of amethyst, seen in my maturity ceremony nearly four years past." Randolf withdrew the amethyst amulet worn on the rough leather cord around his neck, beneath his tunic. She gasped on sight of it, reaching for it, recognizing the perfect match to the one in her own crown. "With this vision of life was also given the countering prophecy of loss. If I lose the star of amethyst, the hunter will become the hunted for all time."

"What does it mean?"

"It means you and I are bound by fate, by the very Creator of the Universe, milady, and if our bond is broken, I will be lost forever."

Her face contorted in uncertainly, but then she reached for him, whispering, "I belong to you Hunter Randolf."

"As I belong to you, Lady Sher."

She gave herself to him in their kiss, and then she stood back to remove her gossamer covers and the crown that was her responsibility to her people. He could not miss the significance as she set aside the light silver crown, inset with the jewel of her rarity among her people.

"After this night, there will be no turning back," he reminded her. "In my culture, lovemaking seals the marriage of our bodies and souls eternally."

"As you say, Hunter." And she came to him.

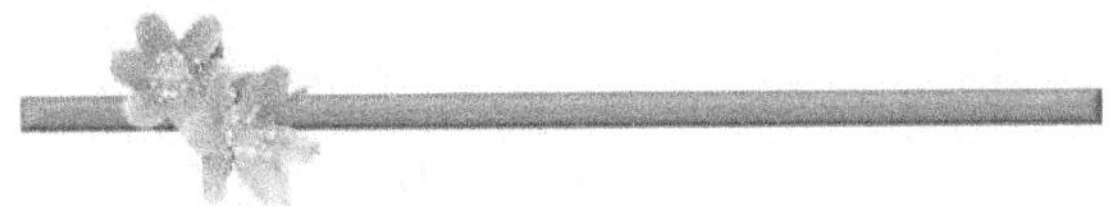

Every touch felt more exquisite than the last. "Randolf," she cried, her own hands stroking the hard muscles of his chest, covered with hair, his back. She understood the cries of pleasure that escaped the couple she'd seen joining in Castaway City. She'd never experienced anything like the waves of joy that crashed over her. She only knew how right it felt to feel it with him alone, to see the emotion in his eyes as returned to her and whispered, "You are my love, my life. I will give you happiness forever, if you are willing to accept it."

"Please. Only you, Randolf, only you I love."

With that, they became one as they danced together, cried together, clasped each other with promises and seals to the fate they'd chosen to accept freely.

Chapter 6

Her body was more sacred to him than the scrolls and runes that belonged to the priesthood of his clan on Chaashane. She curled into his touch when he kissed her shoulder, lingering there with his hand. The emotions he felt were beyond mere protectiveness, mere pair bonding. They had shared the triune facets of love—body, soul and mind. Though he had not impregnated her this first time, his desire to do so would not allow him to walk away from her until he had. Perhaps things would be simpler for them if he walked away before they coupled again, but it was not the Chaashane way. He and Sher were now one. A child borne out of their union would only complete it.

Rising, he went to the window and looked down at the compound grounds. Guarding the staircase to Lady Sher's rooms stood Hunter Bodie. The Patrollers had taken up uneasy vigil below. His brother would not allow them to pass unless an emergency rose.

"Is anything wrong?" her soft voice came to him, and he turned to find her sitting up, looking worried.

Instantly, Randolf went to her. "I have waited for you to awaken so we can love each other once more."

She stole into his arms, opening herself to him on the whisper, "Only once?"

Smiling, he pleasured her with reverence and took the pleasure she bestowed upon him hungrily. Tears filled his eyes at the moment of ultimate joy, the completion of their union, and she wept as though she too realized the extent of what they had done. Faith had been broken with her people. What sacrifices would they be required to make in exchange? And how could they be together the way they were destined?

"My love belongs to you for all time, Lady Sher. No matter what happens without, my heart grows inside you."

She nodded. "I'll never regret loving you, Randolf."

He had but closed his eyes when his instincts rose, danger approached, and a cry rose to his keen ears. *Carnivore.* In an instant, he had dressed and warned her to stay inside with the Patrollers. Inside him, he felt the animal stronger than ever before. Not waiting for his brothers to band together, he chased the Carnivore, knowing it wanted only him to follow. Yet he knew when he had gone, the elders would call for Sher. Would he ever be allowed to see her again?

Randolf could not be sure, but this confrontation with the Carnivore was his destiny. If he discovered the lair and destroyed this particular beast, perhaps the Earth could be saved. Perhaps Sher could be freed from the chains of obligation to love and be with him.

To his great surprise, the great beast led him toward the City of Hope. There, on the outskirts of the City, at last the place the Carnivores entered and departed from like ghosts was revealed.

Numerous and thorough times, the Hunters had been over the same section of the fortress gates. It seemed impossible to Randolf that anything so large could fit between the steel rods. He wondered if the Carnivores possessed some supernatural ability to allow them passage here until he himself passed between with little trouble in pursuit of the man-eater. When he measured the bars, he realized in this area the bars were farther apart. To the naked eye, the gap did not appear larger. The Carnivores' cleverness for illusion disturbed him greatly.

His wrist communicator stopped working as soon as he was through. He was on his own.

The Carnivore stayed just out of his reach, luring him into the dense, humid jungle. Randolf had no trouble slashing through the overgrown mass of vines, but he stopped abruptly when he reached a clearing. In the center of it stood the Carnivore, massive, with white fur and black stripes. It was unlike any Randolf had seen, or killed, before. The eyes of the beast seemed to glow with preternatural wisdom. It was waiting for him, he knew, and then he heard the voice in his head: *I am your destiny, Hunter. As it was foresaw and foretold four years past, the hunter will now become the hunted. You will face me...and lose. Carnivores will rule this planet as we are meant to. Humans will be our food. This talisman you wear will strike fear in the hearts of the Hunters. They will not hunt us again when they realize you are one of us. Then we will be free at last.*

Randolf shook his head. "That will never happen, Man-eater."

As one, they leapt at each other.

Fear forced Sher up, and she dressed, suddenly uncomfortable in her nudity before the Patrollers. They would report back to the elders, if they hadn't already, and they would know she had done what wasn't lawful even, *especially*, for a Queen.

She waited in the hours that followed and the light came. Randolf didn't return. The terror she felt was all new to her, just as their union had been. What if something happened to him?

Swallowing, she placed her hand on her abdomen, imagining a life growing there. A child she could know, could hold, could raise with Randolf in a perfect world. His world, not her own. What would the elders say? Do?

"Patroller, go out. Ask the other Hunters where Randolf is. What's happening? Why does he take so long to return?"

Without a word, they divided into two groups. One group left her rooms, and she waited again in sheer torment for it to return with news. She didn't expect the words it said in her mind. *"You have been summoned to the palace by the elders, Lady Sher of the Amethyst Star."*

"What? What of Randolf?"

"No one knows, Lady Sher of the Amethyst Star."

"No one?"

"No one. You have been summoned by the elders, Lady..."

She rushed out of her rooms and down to the grounds, to The Tank. "Where is everyone?"

When she glanced at the Patrollers around her, their tension as skittish as bugs, she suddenly felt exposed and afraid. They had all gone with Randolf, after the Carnivore. If she stayed, she would be in danger. If she went, the elders would not allow her to return here, nor to see Randolf. Her freedom had come to an end.

But Randolf's child grew within her now. Would the elders dare try to destroy their "half-breed" offspring in the name of protecting all mankind?

Chapter 7

Insects buzzed loudly near his head and the white-hot heat of the sun seared his skin such as he had never felt before. Randolf blinked his eyes against the glare, uncertain of where he was and what had happened to him. His body felt battered. Blood covered his fingers when he swiped at the insects on his chest. He was alone. And the amethyst amulet was gone from around his neck.

When he sat up, Randolf lifted his arms in horror. Black stripes rose against the dark pigmentation of his skin. What had the Carnivore done to him? It had not killed him, but what consolation was that against the growing horror in his mind at seeing the tiger stripes on his own body?

Nothing mattered but Sher. Getting to her before the prophecy of loss came true.

Quickly, he rose and returned to the Hunter Abode. He felt the wariness in his brothers instantly as they surrounded him and he told them swiftly of the means of the Carnivores' entrance and escape. Several patrols were assigned.

Randolf drew Bodie aside. "Where is Lady Sher? Does she

remain here?"

He saw the answer he fully expected in his brother Hunter's eyes. "She was summoned to the palace many hours past, brother Amethyst."

It was as he had feared. He could no longer be one with his brothers. His quest began and would end with Lady Sher of the Amethyst Star.

"What is happening to you, my brother?" Bodie asked, his face tense with worry as he looked at Randolf's arms. Even now the stripes darkened while the skin around them lightened. And he felt his hands curling, the nails becoming longer and sharper. Tiger-like.

"The prophecy," Randolf whispered. "I must go to her."

The prophecy of loss was happening literally. The hunter would become the hunted. If he lost the star of amethyst, he would become a Carnivore. His own kind would hunt him or refuse to and leave mankind to face the Carnivores unprotected. If Sher would no longer accept him, if the elders would not allow their union and their child to survive, the change would be irreversible. He would be lost to his love and his destiny forever as he was hunted like the beasts he'd tracked and killed.

All her life, she'd had no choice. Nor did she now. Sher knew if she submitted to the elders, they would destroy her and Randolf's child. Upon refusing to report immediately to the laboratory facility, she went to her apartment. The elders were waiting for her when she arrived. The voice spoke the instant she entered. "You have done the unthinkable, Lady Sher."

"Yes," she admitted.

"You admit it freely?"

"Yes."

"Why would you do this thing?" the robotic male voice she knew well demanded in a panicked tone she'd never heard used before. "You've endangered your own people, ensured our extinction."

"I don't believe I have. In Castaway City, the humans have pair bonded and conceived naturally. Some of them pair-bonded with Hunters and reproduced as well. The banished city is overrun with children."

"We have heard this ridiculous rumor before, Lady Sher."

"But you haven't gone there! You haven't verified it! It's true. You'll find the truth there."

"You will not leave the City of Hope. You will not leave the palace until you have heard our decision."

They didn't want to know the truth, Sher realized in the hours that followed, hours of silence and torment. They preferred to believe they were the chosen and only purity in their species would keep them alive. They wouldn't go to Castaway City because they feared trusting to anything but the science and politics they'd placed their complete faith in even before the war that darkened their planet. Now, too, they were debating endlessly about implementing new, stricter laws instead of verifying the truth—that their science had failed them.

Chapter 8

No longer could Randolf enter the City of Hope gates on Hunter guard. The change was already too great. Would Sher recognize him?

Stealth he had possessed before the change, and he retained it, perhaps in greater proportion. He slipped inside the city, inside the palace, to her apartment without being detected. She paced the floor but looked up, a scream coming to her lips when she saw him. The Patrollers surrounded her before her scream could fully form.

"I am Randolf, milady!" he insisted, his voice almost unrecognizable. Yet her scream died away. "Believe me, Sher. Stand with me before your elders and pledge yourself and our child to me as I do to you, always. Only then can the prophecy be defeated."

His throat closed. He would not be able to speak again.

"Prophecy?" she murmured, and she gasped as she remembered the words he'd spoken to her earlier. Before she could do more, the doors of her apartment burst open. Hunters poured in, capturing him easily when he gave them no fight.

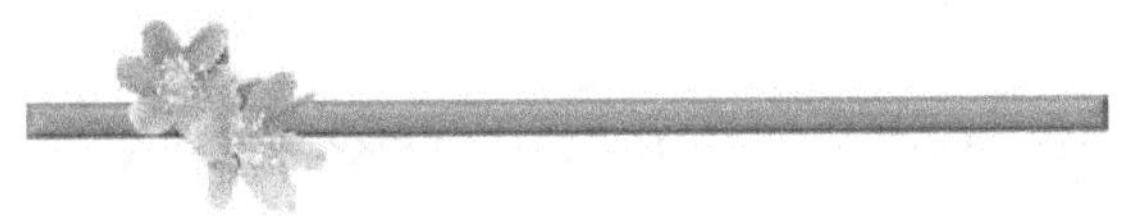

Sher rushed through the Patrollers toward the Hunters. She halted when she saw the Carnivore...white with black stripes, on all fours. But the eyes... Randolf's eyes looking at her sadly, pleadingly. *If the star of amethyst is lost, the hunter will become the hunted.*

He'd changed rapidly, almost beyond recognition. Fearfully, she went to him, sensing the agitation of both the Patrollers and the Hunters, and knelt before him. The tenderness in his gaze, the way he licked her hand, and the quickening of life—half-human, half-Hunter—inside her told her this was the man she loved.

"It's Randolf!" she shouted.

"The prophecy!" some the Hunters murmured under their breath, awed.

Sher turned to the Hunters. "Please, won't one of you go to Castaway City? Bring the children. Bring them here. Bring them into the gates. To the congress. It's the only way to save Randolf." *Save our love and the life of our child.*

One of the Hunters nodded deferentially to both of them, crossed his arm over his chest as he looked at Randolf, then bounded away.

The voice of the elders suddenly broke into the room, reminding Sher that they watched her at all times. They'd seen the Carnivore, seen the Hunters take him captive. "Is Lady Sher unharmed? The Carnivore must be destroyed."

"This is one of our own," one of the Hunters said firmly.

"We can see clearly that it's a Carnivore. It must be destroyed immediately."

Sher rose to her feet, standing beside Randolf. "Regardless of what you see, this is the Hunter Randolf, my life-mate and the father of the child inside me. I won't let him be destroyed. I won't leave his side. You'll have to destroy me, too."

Chapter 9

"Bring them to the congress."

Randolf looked up at Sher and saw the dread on her face. The Patrollers compelled the company within her palace apartment forward, out and a short walk to the congress building. Inside, the huge company of elders—scientists and politicians alike—filled the seats that surrounded the walls of the congressional building. All were male and all were old. Nothing distinguished one from the other.

While Randolf's change had halted—he no longer felt the rapid transformation taking over every part of his body—he knew the halt itself was only temporary. If the elders forbade their union, it would begin again.

"Lady Sher," the voice that had come into her apartment said, amplified throughout the cavernous room, "you have known from the time you became aware of yourself and your surroundings that you were to save your people and maintain the purity of our bloodlines. Our population has dwindled to the point where we cannot survive unless we take every opportunity to harvest precious female eggs and fertilize them only with the strongest male genes we can procure. There is no other way to save our species. We have allowed you all manner of freedoms because you hold the fate of your people in your hand, but we see now that this was a mistake. You have ventured where it isn't proper or advisable for a Queen to venture, not when your value is far greater than the needs of one person, even if that one person is yourself, Lady Sher.

"We have no other choice but to destroy the half-breed you have conceived in savagery. Never again will Queens be allowed outside the palace. Never again will they be allowed the freedoms you enjoyed to your own detriment—"

The massive doors of the congress opened, and a great cry of dismay broke from the elders at the sight of families. Human mothers. Fathers, both human and Hunter. And children, both human and human/Chaashane, flooded in droves that filled the center of the building to capacity. They were the banished. The only free people on the planet.

Among the elders, a cry of uncertainty and shock went up to echo all around the congress. Surely none of them had ever seen the like. Children, given freely by the Creator of the Universe. *Children,* borne in love and reared in love, were the purity and true heart of their survival.

Hunter Bodie and others carried on poles between them the limp form of the Carnivore that had hunted Randolf. Randolf knew the Carnivore was not yet dead—the Hunters would wait to finish it until the elders made their decisions and they knew their brother would be saved. The Carnivore would die, and, with its demise, the power of the prophecy of loss would break. Randolf knew the star of amethyst would soon belong to him for all time, or all would be lost.

Five months later

"Your daughter, milady."

Randolf, no longer tiger but fully himself—the hunter remained the hunter—stood and brought the squalling baby to her mother.

"*Our* daughter," Sher corrected, cuddling the newborn against her bare breast. "Amethyst Star."

Randolf smiled down at them, placing the amethyst star amulet against his daughter. Someday she would wear it. "I have not lost my amethyst star. This is just the beginning, Lady Sher."

She took a deep breath, prepared for anything, so long as he remained at her side.

Seeing the countless families had changed everything. The verification was too much for the elders' faith in the science they'd relied on. With obvious trepidation, they'd agreed to allow interbreeding and pair bonding among any species, even while they continued their attempts to grow children in the lab, with the stock of eggs they'd procured for many years. The fear remained and would remain for some time that this course of action would destroy mankind instead of save it, that a time would come when there were no longer any pure-blood humans. But life on Earth was changing. In Sher's opinion, for the better. Soon all would live together, and in peace, in family units as each individual chose.

"Things are too uncertain here at present, but perhaps when our first set of twins is born, you will accompany me to my home on Chaashane to meet my clan."

She smiled at the thought of having a family. A large family they would raise together with the extended family in his clan. Her home would be wherever Randolf was.

"Are there Carnivores there, Randolf?" she asked uncertainly.

The corners of his mouth turned up. "Only in memories, milady."

Creatures of the Night

Romantic Fantasy

Loner and night-owl painter Susanna Heath has just married her exotic-foreigner husband. Nicholai Rostislav disappears all day, coming to her only at night. Now she finds out that he's a bloodsucking vampire. And you thought your marriage had problems.

Chapter 1

I met Nicholai Rostislav three years ago. I'll probably never forget the first time he walked into my Texas art studio and gallery just minutes before I planned to close up for the night. Any words I intended to speak dissipated. Quite honestly, I'd never seen anyone like him. I was used to bored housewives dragging their cowboy-hatted, rich husbands in to find just the right painting to put over the ranch mantle, musicians looking to immortalize themselves, and professionals needing to decorate or re-do offices.

He was a foreigner—no doubt about that. I knew it even before he spoke. Tall and lean, he had an appealing flush in his prominent cheekbones. With thick, arched brows highlighted eyes so dark and beautiful, he stole my breath in that long minute when he cleared the threshold of my shop and his compelling eyes captured mine.

"Tonight you are open?" he said.

I wasn't sure if he was asking a question or commenting until he added, "I have come by, hoping you would be open, each night for the past two weeks."

My brain had turned to mush. I stood there like an idiot, aware that my face, hands and clothes were already covered with paint, though I'd only begun work a half hour ago.

"I close the gallery closes at 6:30 each night. I'm available by appointment."

My work day began in the evening, just after my only employee left for the night. She handled all my gallery sales. Beyond that she was trustworthy and reliable, I knew nothing about her. The evening was when I did the majority of my painting. Being both a night owl and a loner, I preferred to be active while the rest of the world turned in. I soon learned Nicholai had the same affinity for the night.

"May I then make an appointment for this night?" The hint of his smile revealed brilliantly white teeth.

Could you feel another person's smile inside yourself, as though a butterfly had entered your heart and fluttered wildly to escape from it? I felt like that under his intense gaze. "I…"

"You are Susanna Heath?" He pointed to the bay window with the name of my art studio and galley. My professional credentials as a nationally known artist accompanied the name. Though I preferred a quiet life, I'd opted to stick with the city tradition for established local artists to settle on South Congress Avenue.

I brushed my overly long bangs out of my eyes. "Yes."

"May I look around, Susanna Heath?" he asked, so politely I could only nod helplessly.

If he'd been anyone else, I would have told him to make an appointment with my employee tomorrow. Instead, I nodded, then helplessly watched him walk slowly through my gallery, studying my versatile work with profound interest.

I'd never had one particular focus in my work. I painted in every medium, every style, from rural and city life depictions, nature and wildlife, portraits of the people around me and those who commissioned me. I also did murals and greeting cards. Some of my favorite places to paint at dusk were Mount Bonnell, Zilker Park, and the Hill Country in the spring when the bluebonnets blanketed the hillsides. My work was in both oil and watercolor. Most was done at the request of the buyer. However, I very rarely had shows around the country at various prestigious art galleries. I didn't like to be far from home, nor did I like to be surrounded by people.

This man moved with the grace and swiftness of a cat. I barely heard his footsteps as he took everything in with a single-minded focus that should have prevented him from being aware of my attention. Yet I sensed he felt me as deeply as I felt him.

For many years, Nicholai came and went this way, carrying out with him several of my paintings. Always, he disappeared suddenly for six months or more after his many weeks of nightly visits. I confess, each time I saw him, I was utterly mesmerized by him. The artist in me had painted him a thousand times, but I'd never dared put my brush to canvas. I know my ravenous desire to paint him was all that would exorcise him from my mind, from my thoughts. I fantasized about him endlessly, so intensely that I'd memorized his scent the way a dog might. Sometimes I fancied I smelled him long in advance of his appearance and this alone made my craving for him almost unbearable.

Despite a five-year marriage that'd ended a decade ago, I'd never been in love, never been infatuated, never needed anything that could be described as necessary for every human being. I found myself unable to sleep, unable to eat, roaming the night, searching for peace...for the scent of him nearby. Worse, my work began to bore and aggravate me. My lagging inability to concentrate on anything beyond when I would see Nicholai again made me half insane.

In the third year I'd known him, he returned to my gallery after another six months' absence that knew I might not survive again. He came three nights in a row, and I was certain something had changed, though I didn't know exactly what at the time. That third visit, he came in and I obsessively watched him move around my gallery, wanting something from him that I couldn't define.

"Where do you live?" I asked, trying to make my tone casual and light.

"Romania. My father is Romania, my mother Hungarian. Though I speak many languages, I consider *Magyar*—Hungarian—to be my native tongue."

I hadn't expected that answer at all. I realized, of course, that he wasn't American, but I'd assumed he lived in the United States nevertheless.

"I also have a home here in Austin," he told me. "I alternate between the two."

"That's where you are when you..." *Disappear and leave me destitute.* The instinctive thought brought a flush to my cheeks. The way Nicholai's gaze settled on my face, I would have been willing to bet he read my mind somehow.

If he moved, I didn't notice it in our locked gaze. He was suddenly directly in front of me. "Would you allow me to see your studio...your latest painting?" he asked in a voice so silky, it might have been a form of hypnotism. I was leading him up to my loft long before I realized I had nothing to show him. If writers could have a block where they were unable to write, I as an artist understood it like never before.

I stopped in the open archway that led into my studio. The room had a balcony that overlooked the busy street. Scattered about were countless pieces of antique, sturdy furniture that I alternated between if I was painting a person. Though I'd never been one for excessive cleaning, I tried to keep my studio spotless. I'd, however, long since given up trying to pry up the paint drops dotting the wood floor.

In the center of the room, before the balcony, sat my easel. The look of the blank canvas, all my brushes and paints organized and neat, reminded me of a hospital. Sterile. Ironically, lifeless.

He touched the dry tips of my brushes with his fingertips, trailed them over the white canvas of my easel as if he could backtrack to a time when I was so immersed in my work, the time passed me unawares because I had purpose.

I wanted to tell him I had nothing, I *felt* nothing now for what had given my life meaning and sanity—the passion for painting. But, before I could speak, he was there again, behind me, not touching me, yet I distinctly felt his hand on the curve of my shoulder, against my neck, his arm around my waist, with his granite hard chest at my back. The unique scent of him—spicy aftershave and something else, something old—made me delirious with longing as I drew his essence in with my breath.

"Paint me, *szerető*."

"What?" I faltered at his unexpected request, looking up to see him still in front of my easel.

Impossible. Had I only imagined what I wanted to happen? Did I imagine his caress and the warm of his breath lifting the hairs on the back of my neck? Yet both were distinctly tangible.

"If you have no other engagements, I should like to commission you to paint my portrait, Susanna Heath."

I couldn't speak. Functioning properly was beyond my current ability. All I could concentrate on was the very real impression of Nicholai's fingers brushing my cheek, my hair. The whisper of air came as his mouth brushed mine.

I was losing my mind. Already lost it perhaps, in his prolonged absence. Here I was, projecting my fantasies into real-life sensations. Nicholai hadn't come any closer than before. His arms were at his sides. He hadn't touched me once, ever. Somehow, though, the intense look in his eyes told me I wasn't imagining anything.

"Say yes, Susanna," he said softly, his accent thick and mesmerizing.

What else could I do if I wanted to get my life back? I said yes.

Chapter 2

Painting Nicholai was everything I needed to get over my block. The hours we spent together were some of the most memorable of my sheltered life. Somehow, he was able to stay in the same position for countless hours without seeming to shift even a fraction. I could have sworn at times that we didn't actually say any words during that time I worked, yet each time we ended I knew him better and felt sure I'd parted with some of my own background and secrets. If we spoke, it was only in our minds and with our eyes.

He told me about his family—mother and father, two brothers and one sister. Mother and oldest brother lived "at home" in Romania while the other brother and the sister were restless travelers. Apparently his father had been away for some time, but Nicholai said no more than that he would return at the appointed time.

Against my nature, I found myself telling him about my own loveless family. I hadn't seen my parents for over fifteen years and had no wish to ever seen them again. Though there'd never been any rift between us, I tried to explain to Nicholai, there'd been nothing to hold us together a decade and a half ago when I left home and nothing to bring us back together now.

His shocked response was, *Blood? Love? Do they not create a bond?*

I could only chuckle and shake my head.

Of my ex-husband, I told Nicholai the truth. Stewart and I lived together in companionship, never needing anything of the other, nor truly feeling anything for one another. Stewart belatedly discovered that he did have desires in the last year of our marriage. His affair became serious and he asked me for a divorce. I hadn't reacted when he told me he wasn't satisfied with me or our relationship. I'd calmly told him that I wished them well. To this day, I bore no ill will toward him. The fact was, I hadn't cared enough about Stewart to spare him another thought. We'd lived as strangers, I realized, and my only question was why I'd ever married him to begin with. I didn't like the answer I'd come up with—Stewart was the only person who'd ever accepted me, even if he could never love me.

"What do you love, Susanna?" Nicholai asked out loud, and I looked up in surprise after so many hours of silence.

Had we been conversing? I remembered every word of our conversation this night and those before it, yet his voice in the room jolted me unnaturally.

"Painting," I murmured. "Painting, which I love as deeply as I hate. Long walks. A nice, rare steak."

I expected him to question why painting was my despised obsession. Instead, he asked, "You have no one to share these things with?"

"I don't need to share them."

"Why?"

He sounded so sad, I couldn't help smiling at him. "Because I'm a creature of the night and an alien."

"An alien?" he demanded in surprise. "A foreigner?"

"Okay. It's how I've always felt. I don't know where all the people in this world came from, but I know I didn't come from the same place. I'm like…I don't know, like a dog without a pack."

His disturbed frown made me uncomfortable. "You believe that, lovely Susanna?"

His question wasn't really a question again. I ducked back behind my canvas, but I remembered his words hours later, as the bats in my attic scratched and tried to get settled over my head. *"You believe that, lovely Susanna?"*

I could feel his hands on my shoulders, his lips against the side of my neck.

"Lovely Susanna."

I was alone in the dark, but I felt him as distinctly as if he'd slipped into my bed beside me. I felt his breath against my ear. I closed my eyes as pleasure sharp as pain rolled through my veins like molten lava through a crevasse. I felt his lean, hard body against my back, curve for curve.

"Do you feel this…? Do you feel as I feel, lovely Susanna?"

His words filled my head and I answered him instinctively, from the depths of the misery he'd left me in for so many months. "Yes. Like I've never felt before with anyone else. Touch me."

In the darkness, his hands enclosed my shoulders and then the spaghetti strap of my ragged nightshirt slid down my arm. Dual sensations warred in me when his hot mouth kissed my bare shoulder and his fingertips traced the loose collar of my pajamas.

"The dawn approaches," he whispered.

I took a deep breath and shuddered as I let it out. When I could get myself to open my eyes, I knew I was alone. My fantasy lover had left me in agony once more.

Bitter tears pushed against my eyes. I had to face that this was yet another imagining. Why did they have to seem so real?

Fanatically anticipating Nicholai's arrival the next evening just after sunset, I could feel the intimacy between us even before we spoke.

"Should we get started?" I said quickly to cover my embarrassment. I turned to lead the way to my studio, but those ethereal arms caught me, eased me back into the body I'd only dreamed of touching. Once again, his mouth felt hot against my neck.

"You fill my every waking and dreaming thought, lovely Susanna. I want to touch you."

This isn't real, I told myself angrily at the tears that rose. Not real. But I, literally, felt him so deeply inside myself, I could no longer tell what was real and what was merely a need manifesting itself in fantasy.

More than anything, I wanted to delay the completion of this painting. I'd never taken longer than a month on one project. I couldn't bear to spend more time than that on anything. This one was coming together in much less time. I was born to paint Nicholai Rostislav. Yet I didn't want our time together to end.

I wanted to believe he felt the same when, at midnight, he called our session short to ask if I'd ever walked beneath the moon.

"Often," I confessed. "It calls to me if I don't come." Truthfully, sleep came hard for me. Even when I was exhausted, I could only give in to a few hours. Alone, I felt too vulnerable if I slept longer than usual.

"Then show me the city through your eyes, Susanna."

So we walked. I was painfully aware in the moment he reached for my hand in a protective gesture as we crossed the street that we'd never touched before outside of my fantasies. Unbelievably, this was the very first time. I wasn't willing to break the contact, despite a life-long aberrance of being touched and of touching people. For as long as I could remember, I'd held myself away from everyone. No one had touched me since my husband found his mate in a contortionist with a traveling circus and made me profoundly aware that I was a freak who would always live on the outside.

The bats were, as usual, plentiful, flying out from under the Congress Avenue Bridge and over the Austin sky as we approached the lake. Nicholai asked if I minded them.

"I would never get any sleep, even the few hours I allow myself, without them."

"Pardon me?"

"My attic is full of them. I've gotten so used to their scratching and rustling overhead, I can't sleep unless they're there. And then there's Drac."

"Drac?"

"A bat I had as a...well, a companion. He broke his wing and I mended it. He stayed with me until it healed. He learned to dangle from my finger. I miss him."

Nicholai was smiling when I glanced at him.

"So what do you do, Nicholai?"

"I am a scientist. A geneticist to be more precise, with a special interest in cytogenetics—the specialization of cellular components associated with heredity genetics. However, of late, I have focused on the study of...blood disorders."

"Wow. Sounds complicated."

"It frequently is," he agreed, ending on a deep sigh. "Also frustrating."

"Because your life's work is trying to find what makes anomalies work?" I said off the top of my head.

Surprise filled his face when he looked down at me. "How did you know?"

I shrugged. "I don't know anything about it, but it's just something I've always thought when it comes to trying to cure diseases and stuff like that. It's hard enough to figure out how something works in the standard, but how do you figure out how something works that *isn't* acting the way it's supposed to and normally does?"

"You understand much, Susanna," he murmured appreciatively, and my chest filled with warmth as he squeezed my hand.

"Not really."

"You understand me."

He'd stopped walking, and I did, too, turning to face him.

"Like you, I have always felt I'm a foreigner...an alien, as you call it, and a creature of the night. Unless I'm home and have my family around me, I sense that I don't belong anywhere, with anyone. Only with you I do not feel this way."

I'd never had any experience with being a friend or having a confidante. I'd never been close to anyone in my life, except a pet bat

I'd let go of so he could be with his own kind.

I had no idea how to say any of the things that came to my mind based on Nicholai's words.

I want you to share yourself with me, Susanna, the way you do not feel you can with anyone else.

I heard his words in my head and couldn't convince myself it wasn't real. ...not with the way he looked into my eyes, looking right into me.

I would like to teach you how to live and love life.

I live...

You accept. You stopped looking for a place to belong when you were only an infant.

His insight reminded me of something an aunt, my mother's sister, who lived overseas and whom I rarely saw until she attended my wedding—my only relative to come.

"Instead of holding you when you were a little girl," Maggie told me, "your parents put on the radio and left you alone with the music until it soothed your pain. Or maybe you learned to soothe yourself because they were afraid of you. You're not like other people, Susanna. You must already realize that. You must have sensed how different you are even from you own parents, as am I. So you and I really can't know what love is, can we? We've been loners most of our lives. I've hidden away to keep myself so, but I've never felt fulfilled or whole. From afar, I've watched you. I know that what you have with Stewart isn't love, Susanna. It won't fulfill you. You'll never feel whole with him."

"Then what is it I have with him?" I'd asked, unclear why she would say such things to me on my wedding day.

"Companionship, at best, Susanna. One that won't demand anything of you."

Confused, I said, "Stewart never demands anything of me."

"No. I bet he doesn't. Right now, he doesn't. But I think he will someday, and then you'll know that this isn't love and you were meant for something else."

I had no clue what she was talking about then or why she'd bothered to come today from halfway across the world to try to talk me out of a marriage she seemed to know would fail. Why she claimed to have watched me from afar. I didn't like the disquiet I felt with her. I knew her. At one time, she and my mother had been close, but I hadn't seen her since I was a little girl. A sudden fragment of an old conversation, an old nightmare rose in me: *"Maggie's been bitten. Maggie could die."* I shook it off.

The fact was, I was comfortable with Stewart. She was right that he'd need more someday. That, too, I'd accepted. Never had I needed anything or anyone enough to feel passionately for them. I'd merely accepted, just as Nicholai said now.

What do you want, Susanna?

I couldn't answer. It was like my brain became tongue-tied. What did I want? The obvious—to paint, take walks in the moonlight, enjoy good food. What else was there for an alien who had nothing in common with the other inhabitants around? Until now. Until Nicholai.

Chapter 3

Don't open your eyes.

I gasped on the voice in my head. When I reached instinctively to wipe the tears from my eyes, the darkness prevented me, gathering me in its arms the way it had for the last week.

Nicholai. Each evening, he came to me, I painted him, we talked and, he took everything later. Everything buried deep inside me—so deep, I neither recognized it nor understood it—had risen to the surface at his bidding. When he came to me like this, after he left me physically, his presence appeared in the deep darkness of my bedroom, where there was no light, no shadows.

Nicholai knew me the way no one else in the world—not even me—knew me, or cared to. He alone held me when I cried, and I had no idea why.

You're coming to life, szerető, he whispered in my head.

What is this word szerető?

Lover...

Yes... But, Nicholai...I never died.

Yet I obeyed his command not to open my eyes and realize he

wasn't with me after all. Every morning, I had no choice but to concede that I'd been alone and none of what I remembered had truly happened. Somehow, though, I saw it all in Nicholai's haunting eyes when he came to me in the evening.

Did you not die, my love? Did you not die when you were not held and consoled by your mother or father as a child? Did you not die when they ignored and neglected you out of fear for so many years of your life, leaving you to your lonely destitution? Did you not die when your husband found the love he never asked you for in another woman?

I couldn't give him what he needed. Familiar shame filled me. My own incompetence. I'd failed my husband. *I never knew how. I knew he needed more, but...*

My thoughts were instinctive. I didn't need to speak out loud. Yet the need to make this genuine made me do just that. "I was dead. I couldn't give him anything because I was already dead."

He was right. I'd died long ago. *Life* terrified me for as long as I could remember. The thought of living, leaving my sterile, safe, undemanding existence...

You put all the life you are afraid to live into your paintings. I saw it the very first time I looked into your paintings, lovely Susanna Heath. I saw you, not simply the ghost who drifts over this foreign soil.

I was laid bare, naked, to whom? Somehow I couldn't stand the thought that I was completely alone tonight. I didn't want to see the truth of my life in the stark loneliness of my home. Not when there was no possibility of change. I didn't know any other way to live. Nicholai Rostislav had commissioned me as an artist. He walked with me in the moonlight and held my hand. But the rest was my ghost trying to manifest itself into a corporeal body again. I no longer wanted life if it only meant pain and loneliness.

"You're not real," I said out loud, willing the sense that Nicholai was beside me to dissipate with the chant. "None of this is real."

Every night since Nicholai came back to me from his home in Romania, he disappeared as soon as I opened my eyes. It was, I believed, why he told me not to open my eyes—so it wouldn't have to end between us.

But when I opened my eyes tonight, the bats over my head made their high-pitched squeals and flew like mad back and forth in my attic. I could hear their ruckus as if I was there with them. My head spun and whirled at the sound and the odd sensation that I was falling faster and faster through space. I felt as though I was flying. The landing came hard and jolting. I slammed back into reality— cold, black and quiet as a graveyard.

I wasn't alone. The realization made my heart slam even more fiercely against my ribs. I saw his eyes glistening like diamonds in the black velvet of darkness. Felt the bed beneath me and his arms around me. His lifted his hands and cradled my face. I couldn't function. I was filled with awe and terror. I had to be crazy. This couldn't be real. Yet his hands on me...nothing had ever felt more tangible nor more right.

"What is it you do to me, lovely Susanna?"

"I'm not lovely," I found myself insisting. "I'm not even pretty."

His chuckle sent shivers through the entire length of my body, making it almost impossible to fight my visceral need to tuck myself into him.

"Then why does your face fill my every waking and dreaming thought? Why do I want things I should not? To be what I am, I cannot have what others, even others like me, allow themselves. None of that has ever satisfied me."

"What are you?" I asked, air blocked in my throat.

"An alien. A foreigner. A creature of the night. I do not seem to belong anywhere, not even my beloved home, except with you."

The words slammed against my skull with an emotional force I'd never experienced before. All these nights, I'd had to face what I couldn't bear. If none of it was real, then I truly was beyond hope. Because I could no longer fight the truth. The only place I'd ever belong was with this man.

His face haunted me when we weren't together. I'd been condemned to an existence without pleasure, without companionship since I was a child. Maybe since I was born. At some point, I'd taken up the choice on my own. I'd *chosen* not to feel, not to love. I'd chosen loneliness because I felt so lost and unwanted. If none of this was real with Nicholai, then the choice could no longer be mine. It would simply be my only option.

"The painting..." I murmured uncertainly.

"Yes. I knew from the moment I asked you to do it for me. Only you can complete me, Susanna. Only you can put your life inside it. Inside me."

I tried to draw air, tried to breath, but his words terrified me as nothing else could. If I completed the painting, I would be left with absolutely nothing. Not even the semblance of life I'd allowed myself.

His eyes filled my vision when he came closer. "I never want to leave you, Susanna."

I spoke without considering my words first. "Why do you have to?"

He groaned as thought I'd wounded him. I was afraid, so afraid, but I never wanted him to leave me either. Not when I could have the memory of life.

I touched my mouth to his lips, surprised by how cold they were. I didn't draw back, but instead closed any distance between us and kissed him again. I could feel the warmth gathering in him from the inside out. His fingertips caressed my cheek as his mouth opened beneath mine. The sensation of falling and flying came again. His every caress left me utterly breathless. I'd never know anything like the sensations. I wanted them. I wanted him the way I'd never understood a woman could want a man.

I didn't notice when he peeled my nightgown away. All I experienced was the way his heated kisses brought me to painfully pleasurable life. How could he make me feel so cherished, so beautiful and so needy?

Cradling his head, I almost wished for light. I wanted to see his face as he murmured words I didn't recognize yet somehow knew. This was life. This was love. Real. Forbidden. Meant to be. For all time.

I saw his eyes, reassuring. I shuddered against the force of my own needs.

How could his eyes reassure me even as he kissed me everywhere? My body was no longer my own as Nicholai worshipped it with his lips, sharp teeth and soothing tongue. I thought I might die. Somehow he found me as only he could. Without control, I sobbed when the tension he'd built in me to an unbearable pitch unraveled both abruptly and fiercely.

I reached for him, pulling him up to me. Even while he held my trembling body, I knew it wouldn't be enough. I didn't question my need when I ran my palms over his bare chest, gratified when he growled. Long fingers slipped into my hair, against my scalp in a tingling caress.

I'd never wanted anything like this, even as I'd accepted it in the past as something men desired, and I would hide always afterward for as long as I could. Now I felt no shame and no need to run and hide myself as I murmured incoherently, "Yes, this."

"Susanna..."

"I want you," I found myself begging.

"It could never been enough, my love. Not to fill the cold centuries."

"Yes it will! I'm afraid, too, though."

His eyes again locked with mine. "Flesh of my flesh... I have no soul, no heart. Now you are both, my darling."

"Yes."

He filled me, completed and loved me as though we'd become integral parts of one another.

This act of love bore no resemblance to anything I'd done or felt before. I knew why when he said, "You give yourself to me, *szeretőm*."

I cried without shame or regret until the flying falling sensation ended in a soft landing—his arms catching me, holding me tenderly and endless kisses sent me to the sleep I'd known only as a momentary reprieve, never as bliss and rest.

When I opened my eyes, I knew I was alone. The sound of wings flapped and a familiar high-pitched squeak brought me up and reaching for the lamp beside my bed. I noticed first that I was dressed. I'd dreamed again, but I couldn't have. I couldn't escape the sensation that Nicholai had been with me recently. It couldn't have been a dream.

The flapping of wings returned, and I saw the tiny creature, blind in the light. I quickly switched the lamp off and got up to push aside the heavy curtains I'd put up when night became my chosen haven. I allowed just enough sunlight inside to be able to see the bat.

"Drac," I murmured. He came to me, landing on my finger and dangling from it with his feet. I recognized him at once by the jagged scar on his left wing. "Have you come back to me?"

I gently stroked him. His teeth, now fully grown—nipped at me and drew blood.

When I put him on the curtain rod, I reached for a tissue to catch the copious flood. I saw the note on my pillow then, written in a strange, heavy hand. "He has never gotten over leaving you," it said.

Drac, my beloved little bat? Or Nicholai, who had disappeared from and reappeared unexpectedly in my life for three long years?

Chapter 4

Each time I looked at my painting of Nicholai, I wanted to destroy it, burn it, fling it into the ocean. It wasn't a familiar reaction. My paintings always held me in thrall until they were complete. Then I wanted nothing more than to cast it forever out of my sight. Anything to never have to remember everything that went into it. All of me.

I hadn't seen Nicholai for almost two weeks. At first, I couldn't convince myself I'd dreamed everything that night. The state of my own body from our lovemaking and the note he left on the pillow were undeniably real. Yet angry and agony took their toll on my convictions as night slipped into lonely night.

Maybe I was crazy. My starved mind conjured a lover—one that existed, but only as a client. One who didn't come to finish the painting he'd commissioned me to produce.

I hated him with the intensity I came to hate all my other paintings eventually. I walked, searching for him by sight or scent. I knew even as I despised him for turning me into...what, I knew not. For making me feel, making me love. Dear God, making me *live*.

Night after night, I stared at myself in the mirror, disgusted with my appearance. Hating my straight, outrageously thick, ragged strawberry blond hair. Hating the way it hung in my eyes all the time because I didn't have time to cut it and it grew too fast to keep up with anyway.

I wasn't lovely. I was plain. I knew even if I did as the foreign women around me did, wearing make-up and spending hours with their hair, I would still be plain. Ugly. Unlovable.

How could Nicholai feel anything for me? He'd made love to me out of pity. I easily remembered the evidence of the fact that I was unworthy of anyone's care.

But my self-disgust ended on my withdrawal yet again into an existence without pain, without pleasure. I refused to acknowledge that Nicholai's rejection hurt me so badly because I'd fallen irrevocably in love with him. For that most of all, I vowed never to forgive him.

After the two weeks passed, I received an out-of-state commission that I took without needing to consider. My only dread was that I would and did complete it far too quickly. For once, I had no desire whatsoever to return to my sheltered home.

When I returned three weeks later, I couldn't bear the thought of coming back into my studio. Of seeing Nicholai's unfinished portrait.

I took a cab from the airport to my gallery, opened the door long enough to stow my bags inside. Then I walked out into the night, hoping it would swallow me up so my existence would be tied inexorably to its coming and going. Burned away by the sun...

My hand closed around the scrap of paper I'd carried with me since my dream lover left it on my pillow.

He has never gotten over leaving you.

Did I only imagine you, Nicholai? Alone in the dark after the night we shared, did I imagine you there each night, watching me from the darkest corners of my bedroom. Did I conjure the thought that you wanted to come to me again, but you were uncertain? What did you fear?

I couldn't shake the sudden revelation that I knew almost nothing about this man I loved unwillingly. I understood him somehow. Understood his belief that he wasn't native to this world. He hid himself under cover of the night, the way I did. I understood that he'd resigned himself, as I had, to a life without love, without companionship. Yet why had he told me he wanted me to share myself with him? Why had he claimed to want to be the one and only person to teach me how to live and love life?

He'd taken me out of my numb existence only to thrust me into an Artic freeze, where I might never be warm again. Why?

"Susanna."

The sound of his voice made me turn, and I discovered him walking beside me. I couldn't take it. With a cry, I stopped and ran like the wind back the way I'd come. Ran home and collapsed on my doorstep without the strength to raise myself up and unlock my door.

I hadn't slept in so long, I shouldn't have been surprised to wake and find that I'd fallen asleep huddled against my locked front door. Rain had begun, and its cold had woken me.

My hand against the doorknob, I struggled to my feet while searching my pocket for the key. But as I leaned on the door, it opened with a low, eerie creak that made me shiver. I glanced back, not wanting to see Nicholai yet equally disappointed when I didn't. Had I imagined him by my side again?

Even if I hadn't, I knew I'd done the right thing. I'd been a fool to let myself believe he wanted me, was capable of loving me. I—who had never given myself up to anyone, who'd never allowed anyone to touch me, who'd accepted that to share was to be vulnerable—had committed the unpardonable sin. The only thing I could do was let it go. Free myself from him.

I found myself running into my studio, refusing to look upon Nicholai, even in oil paint. I ascended to my loft above the galley. In my cluttered bedroom, I flipped on the light. Drac hadn't returned from his hunting. I went to the window I'd left open a sliver for him and, after a moment, I closed it sharply.

"Susanna..."

"No!" I closed my eyes to the distinct scene and feel of him with me, behind me, in the room.

Why had I never wondered how he got into my bedroom at night? I'd always been monomaniacal about locking my doors and keeping the world out.

The answer came when I slowly slid my hand into my pocket. My key was no longer there. When I rushed downstairs and out into the pouring rain to check for the key I left in the outdoor sconce, I found it, too, gone. In shock, I realized I'd blindly fallen in love with a madman.

Rage and terror dropped over me when I turned and saw him inside the gallery. His eyes were wounded with sorrow, enough to drown me. I couldn't me as icy cold rain drenched me. I shivered uncontrollably.

"I've been a fool, Susanna. I thought our differences were too great for us to be together. I have no right to ask you to forgive me."

"I don't...want...you...here," I shouted through chattering teeth. "I'll call the police...if you don't...leave."

"Please. Listen to me. If you'll give me that, and if you still want me to go afterward, I promise I shall never bother you again, *szerető*."

I shook my head wildly.

"You'll catch your death of cold, my love. Come inside."

"No. Not until you...leave."

I hated him. I knew I couldn't listen to anything he had to say. I wouldn't love him. I'd rather die.

The sensation that I was falling and flying came again. I tried to fight it. That was when a month of dying caught up to me. I felt myself swaying as my unconsciousness wavered and grew black.

I came to beneath the hot spray of my shower. Nicholai held me up, and I didn't have the strength to fight him. He hadn't bothered to undress either of us, but, when my shivering lessened, he reached for my blouse. I watched him, noticing that he didn't look himself. Gone was the flush of scarlet color that he always seemed to have when he first came to me in the evening. He was pale now, and his skin felt icy even under the hot spray. His lips were completely devoid of color.

Against my own will, I reached for him and removed his coat and shirt. When he stood as bare as I was, I put my arms around him and pressed myself against him. With a shudder, he held me tightly.

"I've been so cold..." he murmured. "Without you, believing we couldn't be together, believing I'd lost you..."

I forced back the sob filling my throat to spit out, "You stayed away. You left me."

"No."

I knew in one simple word, in the look in his devastated eyes, that he hadn't stayed away at all. Each night before I left for New York, he'd been in my room. He'd held himself back from coming to me again. But when he'd come the night I left for my commission, he'd found me gone. Had he returned here each night since, afraid I might never return?

"I wished for death. Without you, I wished only for death."

"Then why did you...?" I started. The tears shoved ruthlessly into my eyes. I couldn't stop them.

"How can I make you understand, my love? I have forbidden all of this for myself, and it simply is not done. How can I have love? How can I give you the love that burns inside me when we are so different? When I am with you, you are the blood in my veins. You make me warm. I have never had those things before. I told myself I could never want them with you..."

"Because I'm ugly. Unlovable."

He wouldn't let me shift away.

"Because you are so beautiful. I have loved you from the very first time I saw you. It was many years past, an art show in New York featuring only your own work."

I knew in an instant. The only art show I'd done in New York was just after my marriage to Stewart. How could Nicholai have known me for ten years without me realizing it? Or maybe I had known it. The first time he entered my shop, his scent was as familiar to me as my own.

"I followed you home when you left New York," he told me. "I watched you for years. Long before I allowed myself to enter your gallery."

"You don't have a business in Austin?" I asked in shock. I'd assumed from the first that his main business was in Romania. A branch of that was somewhere here in Austin, Texas, I'd concluded without the necessary information to come to a solid conclusion.

"No. I come back only for you."

"To watch me?"

"Yes. Never to be with you. But my heart could not be denied any longer. You are my love, Susanna. You are the reason I live. From the moment I set eyes on you, I have wanted you with a passion I refused to believe was possible, even when I realized we could never be together."

I felt his words inside me like living stones, too heavy to carry. "If it's not possible, Nicholai, why did you come back?" I asked softly.

"I have discovered that it is even more impossible to live without you. Still, I know I cannot allow you to be tainted by my world."

"What is your world?" At the very least, I wanted an explanation for why he couldn't love.

Nicholai noticed I was shivering again as the water turned cold. He turned it off and, once outside the shower, dried us both and wrapped me in a robe.

I went to my closet and got another robe for him. "Stewart never liked dark colors," I told him, handing it to him before I picked up the wet clothing. "I'll put these in the dryer."

Moments after I'd dropped them in the machine and turned it on, Nicholai appeared in the doorway in the blue robe that'd been far too large for Stewart, even if he could have liked the color. It fit Nicholai as though I'd bought it just for him.

"Are you hungry?" I asked.

"I have not fed properly since you disappeared."

Neither had I. I'd experienced little if no hunger in the time we'd been apart. "Do you like steak?"

He nodded, and I led the way to my small, functional kitchenette. The table in the center was small and constantly in my way as I moved from fridge to stove, stove to sink. I poured us each a glass of wine before I set about making a hearty meal befitting our lack of late.

"Tell me," I began as I peeled potatoes, "about your world."

"I am no different than you, *szerető*, in my passion for putting all of myself into my work. My life has been my research. My failure."

"Failure?"

"To find a cure."

"Cure?" I asked in alarm, glancing at him. My hand slipped as I chopped the potatoes and the knife slid into my finger. The sight of the blood brought Nicholai bearing a napkin from the center of the table. He wrapped it up so fast, I barely had time to see how bad the cut was. "Do you have a disease?" I asked him, sure no one else would spend their life looking for a single cure if there wasn't a good reason for doing so. A personal reason.

"Not a disease. A genetic...well, disorder. Everyone in my family has had it."

"Is it deadly? Incurable?"

"Not in the way you think."

"I don't understand."

"And I do not know if I can make you understand it, Susanna. But I would not have it passed on to you through our love."

I flushed at his intimate words.

"Is it contagious then?"

"It does not have to be."

I didn't have to repeat that everything he said was beyond my comprehension. He saw it in my face and reached for me, drawing me against him. "I have no right ask you, my love. I cannot lose you again. That I know. If you want me to leave you forever, I am not sure I can. Even if I have to watch you from afar again and that is all I will ever have of you, our memories, I will take it."

I swallowed the warning that filled my throat. *Don't let yourself be vulnerable again.* "What do you have no right to ask me?"

He cradled his cold hands around my jaw, his gaze intensely tender. "I have no right to ask you to be my lover. Be my wife. Never leave me again. Never run from me. I want no fear between us."

When all the strength left my legs at his words, he lowered me to a chair and knelt before me.

"Would you live here?" I asked.

"If you will have me. Or you may come with me to my home in Romania, if you wish it."

"Marry you?" Did I know him well enough? But, if he was a stranger, why did he feel like my very heart? Somehow I'd known he was a part of me for a decade. I'd felt him, longed for him, even recognized him the first time he walked into my shop. At the moment, the only thing I could be certain of was that I couldn't live without him ever again. I was afraid of the changes my existence would take. I knew now, though, that he'd been with me for so long I couldn't be free unless I was with him.

"Marry me. Love me. Give me all of yourself, my lovely Susanna."

"Nicholai..." The words stuck in my throat for only a moment. "I love you. I do. I want to marry you."

"I promise you I will never hurt you or allow anyone to hurt you."

An hour later, we ate and I watched him. While his face remained gaunt, color and warmth filled his cheeks and lips once more. The intensity of his eyes made my fingers uncoordinated. I didn't realize I was breathing raggedly, my thighs trembling, until he whispered my name.

The world around us fell away. In the semi-darkness of my bedroom, he stripped off our robes, his mouth hot and sweet with wine against my own.

"You are more beautiful than anyone I have ever seen, Susanna. Do you know how hard it is not to touch you even before you had met me?"

Only Nicholai. Never had I experienced such joy, such intense intimacy. He was everything. He was everywhere, driving me mad. Even when I felt his teeth, sharp against my skin—but not penetrating it, my excitement only increased.

Uncontrollably, I eased back to see his face. Even when I saw his teeth, piercing his own lip and drawing blood, my satisfaction reached new heights. But when he opened his eyes and I saw pure black—no white at all—there, a jolt when through me that couldn't be explained once I blinked and his eyes were again normal, the blood from his sharp teeth gone completely.

Surely I imagined it. I was in love. I didn't want to be alone or afraid ever again.

95

Chapter 5

We married only two weeks later—in the last place I would have expected. A church. I wasn't sure why, but Nicholai's obvious reverence made me feel unworthy. I felt oddly grateful when he slid an exquisite ring I knew had to be a family heirloom on my finger and kissed me.

For the next week, we spent besotted nights doing all the things people in love and newly married do. We shared picnics in the dusk, listened to classical music while wrapped in each other's arms, read books of poetry and high romance together.

No longer was he gaunt, pale or cold. I felt as bursting with life as he looked. We talked and walked endlessly, and we made love with such frequent intensity, I wondered more than once how I would survive it, and how I would ever get enough of him. Surprisingly, my body always felt brand new each time he reached for me, or the times I simply couldn't wait long enough for him to take the initiative. Even in those instances, he seemed to anticipate me and know what I needed before I asked.

Yet in the daylight hours I spent without him, I found myself uneasy. I had no idea how to get hold of him during these times. Often unable to sleep, I remembered the things we'd done together, usually with a smile on my face. Sometimes, I remembered the way Nichalai's eyes turned black all through when he took release with me. Why did I so easily recall the abundant blood on his lips from his teeth penetrating them, and how the wounds healed so quickly? I found myself both intrigued and repulsed by it. When he was deep inside me, so often I longed desperately to feel his sharp teeth sinking into my skin. I lusted for the sensation of him sucking my blood.

A part of me experienced shame for this. No one had ever made me crave the forbidden, the sinful, like he did. When we were together, I wanted everything and anything he'd give me. Was that what love did to a person?

"Where do you go?" I asked one night, still wrapped in his arms with my back to his front. My skin was covered with perspiration, and I realized I was thinking about the blood on his lips. I wanted to turn to him, taste it, lick it off until it filled me as he still seemed to—everywhere—inside and out.

His breathing sounded ragged. I shuddered at his continued arousal. How could I still want him so bad, as if we hadn't just fallen into each other arm's the moment he appeared tonight?

"I make preparations," he murmured, his tone harsh with desire. "To bring you home with me. Will you come home with me, Susanna?"

A part of me understood that he longed for home just like I did whenever I had to leave. However, in the hours I spent alone here, I'd come to accept that *Nicholai* had become home to me. I didn't like it when he left me, disappearing as though he'd never been there in the first place. I hated being cut off from him.

"Yes," I agreed.

His teeth sank into my shoulder, not deep enough to break the skin. I turned to him and saw just what I craved to see. I crawled over him and covered his mouth with my own. Helplessly, I licked, longing for the sharp, metallic flow I knew would have come if I hadn't kissed him and prevented him from piercing his own bottom lip. I closed my eyes when the blackness completely covered over the whites of his eyes.

Nicholai's nails dug into my back, and a growl issued from one of us—a growl that sounded like that from an animal. My eyes snapped open in surprise. His eyes glowed preternaturally, his teeth elongated—sharp as fangs and brilliant white in the darkness.

Even as I accepted that *I'd* put him in this state with my blood lust, fear overwhelmed me. I collapsed in tears. When he held me so tenderly, I convinced myself I'd imagined his animal growl, that he'd no longer looked human.

The words he crooned to me were unintelligible—I knew he spoke in his native Hungarian—and somehow I felt no comfort this time hearing it. Certainly, I felt no comfort at the thought of leaving my home, traveling across the world to a place I could only imagine as stark and cold. The thought of letting him go there alone, though, only increased my dread. Could his home become mine?

Later, he got up and I heard him a flight below in my studio, pacing restlessly, muttering foreign words in a way that made me wonder if he was angry. At whom?

"How can I have love? How can I give you the love that burns

inside me? I told myself I could never have what I want."

The memory of Nicholai's words compelled me to get out of bed and creep silently down to my studio. I found him sitting with his hands over his face, on the divan I'd painted him on.

My heart wanted to go to him, but my mind told me that he needed more than I could give right now. Silently, I padded to my easel, prepared the paints I needed, and I completed him.

We didn't speak until I stepped back.

"Is it finished, Susanna?" he asked softly.

"Yes, Nicholai. Now we can go home."

Chapter 6

I'd never been outside the United States before. Nichaloi saw my nervousness and distracted me valiantly during the long, dark flight in his private jet. We sat with all the window shades drawn tightly down until the pilot announced that he would make a pass over the Carpathian Mountains before we made our descent in Romania. Only then did Nicholai raise the shutters that covered each window tightly. Though it was night, I saw the impression of a mighty and vast mountain range. I knew this area was steeped in legend, in paranormal whisperings, but I never expected to feel the icy fingers of uncertainty that raked through me.

The thought that I was walking, flying, over my own grave filled me so I barely heard when Nicholai said, "My home has its starkness and its lush beauty."

Less than fifteen minutes later, the plane landed and Nicholai led me to a limousine with dark windows and plush, red velvet seats. He spoke a few words of what I assumed was Hungarian to our driver, then leaned back with me on the seat.

"I have asked my family to give us a week to settle in before they descend on us."

My dismayed expression made him chuckle and hug me close to him. "My eldest brother and my mother live in the castle. They'll remain in their towers until we're ready to receive them. We'll take our meals in ours until then."

Castle? Mother and brother lived with him? With *us*? I wasn't sure how I felt about living with others. I'd been a loner all my life.

But before I could open my eyes to express my concern, I heard the window on my side slid down. Nicholai pointed to the full moon hanging like a gigantic Christmas bauble in a sky draped in grayish-black velvet.

I saw the castle in the distance then and gasped at how imposing it was even from afar. Castle. The image of crumbling stone, merciless cold and drafts, and darkness locked the uncertainty in my throat. But I wouldn't have to worry about seeing my new relatives often. I could only look on in growing horror as we approached the immense, sprawling castle rising over the tremendously tall walls surrounding it. I'd never seen anything more imposing in my life. Nothing about it seemed friendly to me. How could I live here?

"The castle is almost seven hundred feet in length," Nicholai told me. "The walls are battlemented and forty feet high. The stone is gray limestone as well as sandstone—my family has remodeled and reconstructed it several times. We have several courtyards and gardens I know you will enjoy walking with me. Ah, here is the Great Gatehouse."

As we approached the massive gates, a series of howls rose into the night, close enough to make every hair on my body stand on terrified end. Out of nowhere, the massive gray head of a wolf appeared near the car window I leaned out. Instinctively, I recognized it. I felt it inside me as if it were a part of my very being. Never had I seen a wolf this big. It was larger than a bear, silver gray and—I couldn't be sure but—it seemed to be running on its two back legs, only using its front for speed.

When it lunged at me, jaw foaming, Nicholai yanked me back and threw up the window. The wolf hit the pane, causing the glass to splinter. Nicholai yelled at the driver and the car sped up. When I looked behind me, I saw an entire pack of the snarling animals circling and pursuing the car.

Utter terror filled my throat as I huddled against my husband. I closed my eyes, and I heard the whisper of words in my head: *"Werewolves. She's been bitten. The baby's been bitten by one of them."*

My eyes snapped open on my gasp, and I shook my head against the words that felt like actual memory. I saw that we were pulling through the gates. Against my will, I turned back again as the gates closed behind us. Howling furiously, I saw the saliva dripping from the wolves' massive jaws. I saw their eyes unnatural yellow glow in the moonlight. Their incensed growls filled me until I felt like my insides vibrated with them.

There was no escape.

Chapter 7

"What were those things?"

"I told you we shouldn't have left the States. I told you we shouldn't have left home, especially with Susanna so young," my mother wailed. "Maggie could die..."

But my father wasn't listening to her. He was holding me and demanding of the old man sitting in front of us, "What were those things?"

"Vérfarkas. Werewolves," the heavily accented voice said, then added something in another language.

"Maggie's been bitten then. The baby's been bitten by one of them!" my father whispered in horror.

"But this is not fatal. This is only a scratch, you see? A surface wound. This little one will not change, become, like your sister will, madam, not until she is bitten."

"What do you mean 'until'?" my father demanded.

"This little one will not feel whole until she becomes one of the pack. She will be hunted by them always. She will recognize them as brothers. When they call her, she will go to them. The gene has already

entered her bloodstream."

"There is no cure? No treatment? No way to change this?"

"No, no cure, except that she be bitten by a vampire!" The old man cackled at that idea.

"Dear God..."

I woke to a place I had no recollection of until Nicholai rose from the fireplace, replaced an andiron and came to me on the elaborate, velvet-curtained and covered bed. I remembered then that I'd been so distressed by the changes in my life and the...the werewolves, I'd wanted nothing but to immerse myself in my husband's love and to sleep until the memories faded. I'd dreamed of my aunt Maggie and that trip my parents had taken overseas when I was just a little girl. It was a memory buried so deep inside me, I wanted to believe it wasn't real. Just a story. Just a tragedy that meant nothing to me.

"I'm sorry," I said when he lay beside me and kissed me.

"I am sorry for nothing, my love. I have only dreamed of you here with me."

He'd dreamed of me, Susanna Heath, woman afraid of the world, not whole, not fulfilled, not worthy of even my parents' love. I was aware of how undeserving I was of his happiness to have me here.

"How long did I sleep?" I asked.

"Twelve hours. It was a long flight. And I so thoroughly exhausted you upon arrival."

His smile put tears in my eyes. I hugged him fiercely. He was my home now. Would he leave me all those hours of daylight even here?

"Are you hungry, *szerető*?"

His question made me realize just how ravenous I was. My

stomach answered for me with a long, hollow roar.

Chuckling, he got up and used the intercom near the door. No, I decided upon looking around, this most certainly wasn't a castle of old, though I could see it'd been standing for a long time. I remembered Nicholai telling me upon our arrival that it'd been fully modernized with every conceivable convenience.

I noticed the small bat house we'd brought Drac overseas in was empty.

"Do…do you have servants?" I asked in surprise, realizing after he'd asked someone to bring food that it meant someone would be serving us. I rose from the pillows.

"Yes. Many of the gypsies that surround the castle work for us. Should you ever need anything… But then the gypsies do not speak English. If you need anything, ask me, my love."

"Does that mean you'll be with me always?"

He came back to me. "This is our honeymoon, Susanna. But soon I will need to return to my research, and you will be longing for your painting. I have prepared a studio I hope you will love, but, first, we have time for a luxurious bath before we eat."

Nicholai led me through the bedroom I decided was large enough to be an entire apartment on its own. It was filled with furniture that seemed too rich and elaborate to believe came from this era. My loft resembled a cardboard box with wood blocks for furniture compared to this luxury.

The bathroom was nearly as large and extravagant. The thoughts I'd had of a cold, dark, crumbling castle fled at the sight of the fancy toilet (why did that seem like an oxymoron to me?), and the square, marble surrounded bathtub large enough to fit four. All around it were gold pipes, taps and buttons. I watched as Nicholai filled the tub with steaming water and fragrant bubbles while I cleaned my teeth with the obviously new brush hanging in the gold stand above the sink.

I remembered him saying he'd prepared for the hope that someday I would come home with him.

"Are you rich, Nicholai?" I asked in surprise.

"My family has everything we need and more," he agreed. "Are you not also, Susanna?"

I lived like a monk, true enough, while my "gold" accumulated almost effortlessly from my painting. I didn't see any reason for living more extravagantly when I could accept a simple life just as readily.

"How long have you been preparing for me to come here with you?" I asked when we slid together into the gloriously hot water.

He drew me across the length of the tub and into his arms. "For as long as I have loved you."

Guilt filled me and warred with my overwhelming love for him. What if I couldn't stay here? What if I couldn't bear being enclosed in these massive gates for long? What if I wanted to leave?

"If we go, we go together," he said as though he'd just read my mind.

I wanted to say something, but I didn't know where to start.

"Listen to me, Susanna, and heed me, I beg of you."

I would have to be deaf and blind not to recognize the earnestness in his tone and in his expression.

"This area where I live can be treacherous. Sheer cliffs that sneak up on you before you realize how close to the edge you are.

The vast, dense forest that harbors...all manner of creatures."

"Creatures? You mean the wolves?"

"Wolves, but not wolves. *Vérfarkas.* They are bloodthirsty. They will try to lure you to them. They have killed many hapless travelers and gypsies. They have no concern for life. You must not leave the castle without me."

"But they can't get through the wall, can they? It was as tall as it was thick, or nearly so."

"There are posterns—gates—in and out, but they are locked. They will try to lure you to unlock them."

"A wolf?" I said in disbelief, but the terror of the past—the terror that seemed to be back again—hung in my throat.

"*Vérfarkas. Were*wolves, Susanna. They do not come into the posterns because they have had no reason to in the past."

I didn't understand what he meant, and I had little time to think of it over the next several days as Nicholai gave me a slow, thorough tour of the castle. The plushest hotel in the world couldn't begin to rival it. Nicholai showed me all the rooms in our tower—the bedrooms, library, sitting rooms, reception hall. He led me through the upper, middle and lower baileys, the upper and lower great hall, the lesser hall, the dungeon he used for his many-roomed laboratory, the kitchen with the buttery and pantry, the chapel and the barbican that was an extension of the castle gateway. Nicholai spoke about the architecture and design specifics as though he remembered each detail or had himself built the castle from the ground up.

Despite the modern conveniences everywhere, the castle halls and rooms were dark. Most of the windows were covered in heavy drapery that effectively kept out even a single ray of light. I'd never seen anything like Nicholai's home.

Finally, saving the best for last, he said, he led me to the art studio he made for me. The tower room itself was exquisite. It opened out to an absolutely enormous balcony that overlooked the landscaped lawn and many gardens below that gypsies tended each time I looked out. More than that, the view of the dark, lush forests surrounding the castle—the forests Nicholai had warned me about—spread out to the left and right as far as the eye could see. The view of the rolling valleys that seemed like a vast green carpet presenting the mountains was exquisite. I wanted only to set up my easel on the balcony and satisfy the starved artist inside me by painting everything around me from every conceivable angle and viewpoint.

But Nicholai steered me away from the balcony to show me the supplies he'd had shipped here for me. I marveled over the finest materials and paints, enough to last me a year or more. Unbelievably, he said, "If you need anything more…"

I shook my head. For the first time, I felt I could be happy here— with him—happier than I'd ever been in my life.

Chapter 8

Meeting his family had been an apprehension in my mind since Nicholai mentioned it. I held little emotion for my own family, but I knew his love for his was boundless. I sensed it each time he spoke of them. I didn't understand the situation with his father, however. He'd told me his father had gone away and there wouldn't return for many more years—"in the next age." I assumed he'd died. Yet Nicholai showed no grief about this. Again, his reverent spiritually unnerved me.

"Did he die of the genetic disorder your family has?" I asked.

"Our genetic condition does not cause death. Quite the contrary. Father has not chosen death. He will return at the appointed time."

This made no sense to me, but I didn't press it. Maybe someday I would understand Nicholai's ways.

"I have nothing to wear," I told him while standing before the pitiful excuse of a wardrobe I'd brought with me. All my life, comfort had been my only concern. Frequently, I'd forgone clothing at all while in my loft and studio. Nudity was the most comfortable state of being, after all.

Nicholai moved over to me and pushed open the door of the immense closet next to mine. I'd assumed it was empty.

"These are yours, my love," he said simply.

I stared in silent shock at the seemingly unending row of clothing in colors I'd never dared to wear, believing black and gray cotton was all I needed.

I gingerly touched the exotic, bright fabrics.

"My mother and sister have had great pleasure in choosing your wardrobe. But you are under no obligation to use any of it. I wanted you to have everything you needed here."

I'd had no great love for designer clothes until Nicholai left me to dress for dinner with his family. Pearl-encrusted, silk, satin, velvet, elegant pantsuits and dresses so beautiful I wanted to try on everything at once. But I knew his mother and brother were waiting.

I chose a deceptively antique, rose-colored dress with beadwork and a flouncy hem. I was convinced it either wouldn't fit me or wouldn't look right on me. I was wrong on both counts. The dress fit as thought made for me. Once I found a pair of matching ankle-strap sandals, I could hardly believe it was me standing before me in the mirror. Wearing color instead of black or gray made my skin look creamy instead of uneven.

Though I didn't know the first thing about either, I applied a touch of the make-up I'd found in the bathroom and I pulled my hair up into a loose ponytail with my over-long bangs framing my squarish face.

Uncertain of myself, I passed up the silver on the right of the jewelry box on the vanity and instead added a pair of gold hoop earrings to my dress. Not for one moment had I envisioned any of this for myself before now.

When Nicholai returned for me, my confidence in what I'd done floundered for a moment as he gazed at me in surprise.

"No other woman steals my heart and my breath so easily as you do, Susanna Heath," he murmured reverently.

I took the steps to him and reminded, "Susanna Rostislav, if you please" with a hint of a smile.

We walked down to the elaborate dining hall, and just before we entered, I asked whether his family spoke any English.

"Of a fashion," Nicholai told me. "They have never been to the States. You may find their English heavily accented."

He wasn't kidding. His brother Viktor was all but unintelligible as he bent over my hand and kissed it. His smile and good looks told me he was a flirt—and the committed bachelor-womanizer Nicholai told me privately he was with the gypsy women.

Their mother surprised me most. Marika, I was convinced at first sight and every one afterward, couldn't have been older than thirty-five. Her face was unlined, not a single wrinkle. Her voluptuous body in a rich velvet dress couldn't have belonged to a woman who had to be much older than my thirty-six years.

She came to me, her eyes so like Nicholai's, filled with tears. Her accent thick, I nevertheless understood her because she spoke so slowly. "Susanna, I have so longed and waited to meet the woman who has held my youngest son's heart in misery all these many years."

Misery? I didn't know what to make of her greeting. Her adoring smile in my direction only confused me more.

"Unrequited love can cause the worst kind of misery, beloved," she said, obviously seeing the uncertainty in my face.

She lifted my chin, brushed my hair from my eyes, then took my hands in her own. "Welcome to the Castle Rostislav, Susanna. Welcome to our family."

She kissed both of my cheeks, beaming at me with such happiness, I immediately felt part of the family. Marika's eager questions, Viktor's flirtations, and Nicholai's proud admiration and frequent caresses convinced me that I did belong here.

Only later, wrapped in each other's arms and in the velvet darkness, did a chill run through me at Nicholai's whisper, "I cannot bear the thought of losing you, my love. We have so little time."

"What? Do you expect me to die first?" I joked languidly.

He didn't answer, and I knew he did indeed expect me to die sooner than he did.

But I didn't want anything to spoil my newfound happiness. I put all but joy out of my mind.

Chapter 9

Days slipped into weeks and then months. My bliss turned into a sort of restlessness and unease that couldn't be applied to any one thing. Rather, the accumulation of odd events made me feel the uncertainty I'd come here feeling.

My painting fulfilled me as never before. But, as I gazed out at the mountains in the distance—mountains I'd perfectly transferred onto my canvas—my gaze continuously and uncontrollably went to the forbidden forest. Nicholai had warned me about going into them, of ever leaving the castle without him. He'd warned me that the werewolves—beings I staunchly refused to believe existed—would try to lure me to unlock the gate to them. On the long walks we took each evening, Nicholai wouldn't allow me to get close to the wall, let alone to the wrought iron, locked gates set inside it at intervals.

Since Nicholai had returned to his research only days before, our nightly strolls through the many courtyards had become less and less of an occurrence. It was almost beyond bearing to stay inside when I felt I needed to be outside. I couldn't explain the calling I felt to leave the castle. Nevertheless, I heeded my husband's worry and stayed inside.

I saw Viktor only at meals in the Great Hall, and Marika came to visit me often. I'd grown to enjoy the time with her. However, I couldn't deny that the lack of aging I saw in her disturbed me greatly. Additionally, I discovered that Nicholai wasn't the only one vague about his father's absence. Marika spoke of her husband often, her words and face filled with love, adoration and loneliness. She, too, insisted that he would return to her someday, at the appointed time. It made no sense to me. It was clear none of them had any contact with him, yet they acted as though he was still in the castle somewhere and they never saw him. It got to the point where I couldn't bear to hear my mother-in-law speak of her longing for her husband anymore. I took to wandering the castle to avoid her. This caused me guilt because she and Nicholai had made me feel such a welcome addition to their family.

One day, I discovered a second library Nicholai hadn't shown me when he gave me a tour of our tower. This one was smaller than the one near my studio near the top of the tower. On the desk of this strange library, I found a book that looked like a personal journal. When I flipped through it, I recognized Nicholai's handwriting, though I'd seen it before only in the note he'd left on my pillow long ago and on our marriage license. I was frustrated about the fact that he wrote in what I assumed was Hungarian. It wasn't right of me to read his private journal, of course, but my annoyance couldn't dissolve the guilt. I wanted to understand my beloved husband, understand the strange things he did and said sometimes. I wanted to understand how he could simultaneously confuse and illuminate me, scare and comfort me.

A scurrying noise caught my attention. I glanced up, frowning, and a scream lodged in my throat. Before it could escape, the vision above me disappeared. I ran out of the room and out the nearest exit. The courtyard spread out in front of me in a grassy, two-hundred-foot-square—the courtyard nearest the gate, which Nicholai had called a postern, leading to the forest.

I shook my head, telling myself I hadn't seen what my eyes told me I had. Nicholai's mother had been on the wall above me, near the ceiling. She'd been crouched on all fours, somehow holding there as she watched me, much the way a spider perched on a web would. By all accounts, she should have fallen, yet she remained easily. Her eyes had been black through and through, like Nicholai's sometimes were.

Realizing I trembled violently, I considered going back inside for a coat. Somehow I felt safe out here in the sun.

I forced myself to walk off the scare by circling the castle. As I passed the gypsy workers, I nodded to them. They were polite, but something in their dark eyes told me they didn't trust me.

As I came back around the castle to the place I'd come out, I found myself ignoring Nicholai's warning. Why would the werewolves try to lure me if they had no reason for ever coming to the castle before?

I went to the gate-like door that led outside of the thick walls surrounding the castle. I'd never gotten this close to the forest. I recognized the strange longing inside me as I stared through the wrought iron bars of the postern. I wanted to paint the forest. I didn't want to be above it, as I was in my balcony studio. I wanted to be on the ground, facing it, trying to capture the hidden things that lurked inside that thick blackness.

The unnatural sound of a wolf's howl came so close that I jumped back from the gate. But I wasn't in time to avoid the swipe of the creature's claws. I felt the scratches it left behind even though my eyes were locked with the yellow ones staring at me from outside the gate. As I backed away, I recognized the burning, the itching of the scratches. *"This is not fatal. This is only a scratch, you see? A surface wound. The little one will not become."*

I turned and ran back into the castle. Oddly enough, the scratches healed only an hour later, leaving behind almost indistinguishable white marks like those faint markings I'd had on my chest as long as I could remember.

Something felt different between Nicholai and me that night, something I couldn't explain. His questions seemed too targeted. If he'd been in his laboratory in the dungeons, how could he know where I'd been and what I'd done earlier that day? Unless his mother *had* been on a spider on the wall of his private library.

Chapter 10

"The vérfarkas *come to the very walls, the way they have never dared before. I fear for Susanna, knowing what lurks inside her. Knowing how cunning the* vérfarkas *can be. How bloodthirsty. Yet I know it is more than that. She is like them. I have discovered in the two tests I ran of her blood back in the States that she has the* generatív szakasz (növ) *they possess. I have asked Mother to look after my beloved, but Mother believes Susanna is frightened of her, may have seen her spying. And Susanna's curiosity about the forest and of her own kind—despite my warnings—must be stopped. How can I convince her to trust me?"*

I'd spent the morning and afternoon in Nicholai's private library on the second floor, trying to translate the last entry in his journal. Some of the translations of the words weren't clear in the Hungarian-English dictionary I'd taken out of our own library in the upper levels of our tower. I couldn't translate these words, and my frustration mounted as the afternoon wore on.

Greatly disturbed by what little I'd deciphered, I wondered what it all meant. Nicholai had called the werewolves *vérfarkas*. Were werewolves real? I found it difficult to accept. Were they capable of predatory behavior, rather than simply instinctual? Nicholai seemed to imply that I was like the wolves in some way—"what lurks inside her", "her own kind" and "the same *something* they possess". *Generatív szakasz (növ)*, as I translated it, was a stage in the reproduction cycle. I didn't understand how Nicholai used it in his journal entry.

Was it true the werewolves were hunting me? That they had been hunting me all my life?

I also noted that Nicholai had used the word "dared", as if the wolves were subject to his rule. And his mother was spying on me—perhaps I hadn't imagined that, even if my memory of her spider-like antics on the ceiling couldn't be real.

The scuttling sound that'd drawn my attention yesterday in this very room came again, and I only had the briefest glimpse of Marika crawling along the ceiling on all fours like a lightning quick arachnid.

Strangely, my first concern was that she would tell Nicholai that I'd been trying to read his personal journal. What would his response be? I had to know. I needed to know! Compelled, I ran through the shadowed castle halls to the dungeons one floor below. Long before I arrived at his laboratory, I heard him and his mother talking as though they stood directly next to me.

"How long will you keep your secret, darling?" I recognized Marika's thick accent.

I didn't question why they spoke in English when alone together. Nicholai had told me before I met his family that, since he had told them of his marriage to me, they made every conversation one in English in order to improve their skills in speaking it. Each time they were together, I heard them only conversing in English.

"I have no wish for her to know, Mother."

"If you do not tell her and if you do not give her the choice, you will lose her. It is that simple. She is mortal. I have gone to the sleep far longer than she has been on this earth. Would you not live forever with her, my son?"

"I could not make her *this*!" Nicholai all but shouted. "You believe we are God's agents to rid the world of evil. If that is true, why are there so few of us, Mother? And why is evil allowed to flourish? God did not commission us, much as our family wants to believe it to be true. Perhaps believing this is what keeps us sane throughout the endless ages, when the sleep is all that sustains us indefinitely. That, or the burning..."

"Do not even speak of it!" Marika shrieked, and I cringed back against the wall. "I will not lose you as I lost Nadia. Perhaps if she had chosen love as you have, your sister would not have walked into the sun to end her time."

In the silence that followed between them, I instinctively held my breath. Nothing they were saying made immediate sense to me, yet I knew I couldn't slip away now. Not until I'd heard it all. I needed this.

"I fear when mortality claims your beloved Susanna, you will also see no other recourse but the burning," Marika said softly. "It does not have to be this way, Nicholai. She will love you—for all time! Yes, certainly that, now that your child grows inside her."

Dead silence blanketed the blackness soft as velvet around me. I'd grown so used to the darkness in this place, I'd forgotten the fear of it. Until now. Now it felt heavy and menacing as I waited in the breathless silence. Shivers of terror moved up and down my spine.

"*Strigoii* do not conceive, Mother," Nicholai said on a sigh. "There have been no children in our family since you and Father were reborn with the dark gift of immortality."

"You know why this is so, Nicholai," Marika insisted with more enthusiasm than seemed warranted. "Susanna...she is mortal. She is the only mortal who lives and remains with us. Immortal cannot conceive. Mortal can."

My hands went instinctively to my womb, as if I could feel the life growing there. Had I known before Marika spoke it? I'd told myself stress had driven my period into hiding.

"You must give up this nonsense. Finding a 'cure' for what we are, Nicholai. Accept our gift, as all your family has—"

"Not Nadia! Never Nadia," Nicholai fiercely, as if his sister's choice somehow proved his point.

Somehow, I sensed the pain his words inflicted on his mother. I heard it in her tone when she said, "All that matters now is your wife and your child, my son. You must protect them. You know the *vérfarkas* sense her."

The word Marika used suddenly became familiar to me. It was the very word I'd spent most of the day trying to translate in a way that I could understand and believe! The very same word Nicholai had used for werewolf—the creatures that Nicholai insisted would try to lure me. The bloodthirsty, cunning animals *I* was like—biologically. I possessed something in my blood that they, too, had. Nicholai had confirmed this while in the States.

I remembered Drac—who now flew about and without the Castle Rostislav freely—biting me...drawing copious amounts of blood that I'd finally stemmed with a tissue I'd tossed in the trash.

Had Nicholai retrieved it and tested it, only to find something he dreaded? Then again, when he came back to me after the endless absence that nearly claimed my sanity, I'd cut my finger slicing potatoes. Nicholai had wrapped it in his handkerchief...and taken it with him. Perhaps there'd been no mistaking this time—whatever he'd found in my blood before proved to not simply be an anomaly.

I hadn't wanted to accept the werewolves' nearness when I took my walks around the castle grounds. The creatures were just beyond the wall, sensing me as I sensed them. Hunting me. Luring me.

A noise came from the lab, and I realized either Nicholai or Marika were coming out. On bare feet, I rushed away without a sound. I stopped only when I closed myself in the bedroom I shared with Nicholai. Sitting on the edge of the four-poster bed, I tried to calm my racing heart.

What had I heard? What had Nicholai and his mother talked about? My confusion was so great, my mind was already hard at work confusing all until nothing but a jumbled mess remained. Only two things stood out in stark uncertainty. They'd referred to me as a mortal and to themselves as immortal. How was such a thing possible? If not mortal humans, what were they?

Ridiculous! Surely I just misunderstood everything. Yet the memory of Nicholai's black eyes, the unnatural look of him that day that felt long ago now when I'd longed to lap up the blood on his mouth came to me. The growl I couldn't trace to its origin. His mother's wall crawling, the way he was always with me, yet not there when I'd barely knew him yet craved him so intensely. The way his family disappeared in the daylight hours. The way Nicholai touched me when we made love, the way I always felt his caresses everywhere all at once...

My stomach tightened. *"Susanna will love you—for all time! Yes, certainly that, now that your child grows inside her."*

Protective instincts rose inside me at the thought of a child growing inside me. A baby Nicholai and I had conceived together. *Mortal and immortal. Human and...what?*

The bedroom door opened abruptly, and I jumped at the sight of Nicholai. The way he looked at me made me poignantly aware that I'd fallen in love with him so irrevocable, fallen in love with who? With *what?*

"Are you all right?" he asked, coming to kneel before me. When he took my hands, he exclaimed, "You're freezing. Let me get a fire going, *szeretőm.*"

I didn't protest, merely watched him uncertainly at the fireplace. Then I asked, "What does that mean? *Szeretőm?*"

Nicholai smiled at my awkward attempt to mimic Hungarian words that didn't roll easily off my tongue. *""Szeretőm' means 'my lover'."*

Before he came to me, he called down for hot tea. Then he led me to a comfortable chair before the fire. He kneeled beside me as I closed my eyes to enjoy the warmth of the roaring fire.

"I am worried about you, Susanna."

"Why?" I asked, my voice only half there as I stared at this man I loved almost to the point of pain. Was he a stranger?

"Perhaps we should return to your life in Austin. Winter will be coming soon, and it is much colder here than anything you have ever known."

"What about your research?" I asked in surprise.

"Nothing matters to me except you, Susanna. I only want to make you happy. I desire only to take care of you."

I no longer knew what to believe. Everything in my life had ceased to make sense. Especially the strangeness of love.

Chapter 11

I woke on the edge of the forest and blinked against the sunlight fading into a purple dusk. I heard what, at first, sounded like nothing more than incoherent shouts. Then my own name became familiar in the heavy brogue issuing from more than once source.

When I lifted my head, pain such as I'd never experienced before seized me. Of its own volition, my hand went to my throat, and I drew it back to see blood, black and sticky. The sight brought a burning at the edges of my consciousness. Why did I remember Nicholai calling for me? I remembered that old, familiar sense that he was with me when I knew he couldn't be. What had happened since then?

I came to again with hushed voices near me.

"...risked the burning to save her! You must feed, my darling son. It is the only way to ensure—" Marika pleaded desperately.

"I will not leave her, Mother! Not now, when she's received the bite," Nicholai's voice came, harsh and unyielding.

"Then drink from me. You will frighten your beloved with your appearance if you do not regenerate with my blood."

I closed my eyes, afraid to open them and see what Marika meant. But I couldn't prevent myself when I heard a wet sound, a slurping sound.

Surely I imagined it! Nicholai, horribly disfigured. Blackened. Burned. Surely I imagined the sight of him with his mother's wrist pressed hard against his mouth.

When I came to again, Nicholai looked just as I'd always loved him, sitting beside our bed in a chair. He held my hand.

His careworn face came closer. He seemed unduly relieved to see my eyes flutter open. "Susanna, tell me how you got outside the wall!" he demanding, astonishing me. "I was beside myself when I could not find you. I had the gypsies searching the grounds until one of them saw you through the postern. Saw you just outside the forest, where I asked you not to go."

"I..." I tried to remember how I'd gotten there. For I *did* remember being there, reaching up to touch my throat and coming back with fresh, black blood. I'd gone for my walk, as I'd become accustomed to doing during the day, when I was alone for so many hours and my painting began to vex me because I so wanted to go out to the forest...

I had...yes, I remembered that I'd taken my sketchpad outside with me, believing I'd use it when I sat to rest during the turns around the castle. I knew deep inside I had no intention of sketching the gardens, courtyards or the stone walls. My only thought was of fixing the forest in my mind on ground level with a sketch I could later use to fill in my memory for a painting. I remembered putting my hand on the gate handle, unlocking it, hearing the sound of a wolf howling so close by, hearing Nicholai calling for me once again, his ethereal presence. Then nothing.

"I don't know," I managed hoarsely. When I tried to turn my neck to face him, the pain I'd felt before flooded all through me. Tears stung my eyes.

"She's been bitten by one of them! She will change. She will recognize those who hunt her as brothers. When they call her, she will go to them. The gene has already entered her bloodstream."

"What's happened to me, Nicholai?" I asked, weeping. I asked about what happened recently and what had happened to me when I was only a small child. Somehow, he knew. I believed through and through that he knew what I was. What I might become. Because he was one and the same?

Nicholai slid from his chair and into our bed without jostling me at all. "I'll take care of you, *szerető*. I promise. I'll never let you out of my sight again."

But I was sure then that he understood it was already too late for that. I would become. And there was no way to change what was to happen.

My mind filled with the image of Nicholai feeding from his mother's wrist. Had I been bitten by a werewolf? I wondered suddenly. Or had I been bitten by an immortal—my own husband?

Chapter 12

I'd been bitten, but I couldn't be sure by what. A werewolf or a *strigoii*—a vampire? I'd stumbled onto the fact that my husband and my new family were all vampires. But I couldn't get myself to accept it, even when I verified the translation of the word Nicholai had used to refer to himself and his clan.

Over the next few weeks, I had only a few lucid moments when I lived in terror of what was happening to me and the baby I knew I carried inside me. A high fever kept me delirious most of the time, accompanied by unnatural paleness and the sense that my body was restructuring itself from the inside out. The pain was nearly unbearable. My only means of coping with it was the unnaturally deep sleep that claimed me nearly all the time now.

Nicholai remained beside me each time I looked for him. I could see his terror, though it confused me more about what was happening to me.

In my delirium, I often heard Nicholai and his mother or brother arguing.

"She has been bitten," Marika said angrily one time. "If you do not give her your blood, you will lose both her and the child. Only your blood can save them both."

Had Nicholai given me the vampire bite, I wondered, and now regretted it?

"And condemn them to an existence such as this? Taking life as a means of survival?"

"Yes, to survive. Taking *evil* life, as we are meant to by God Himself. We are His agents. Why must you question this when you do not question that we have belonged to Him alone since we were reborn?"

"I cannot do this to Susanna—not without her choice."

"She is already changing. Shifting. Soon, there will be no turning back."

Another time, I heard Nicholai's brother speaking and caught only two words: "awakening" and "Father".

I woke one morning, alone and unexpectedly lucid and strong. I thought of none of the strange things I'd heard. I thought only of food. The kitchen was deserted, and I opened the freezer to find a thick, red steak. I put it in the microwave to defrost, wanting it hot, like fresh meat, but still raw. It wasn't until I finished my meal in no more than a minute and saw what resembled blood covering my hands that I realized what I'd done.

I heard footsteps. Nicholai shouted my name. Quickly, I washed my hands and face.

The wild look on his face dissolved when he saw me and sighed in life and death relief. "What are you doing out of bed, my love? You are not well."

I didn't feel ill, not as I watched him come to me. Lust, hot and full-blooded, rushed through my veins. "I was hungry," I admitted.

"I could have had something brought up to you."

Had his mouth ever looked so lush and red and sensuous to me before? I was mesmerized by it. I reached for it before I was fully aware what I was doing. I felt him stiffen in surprise and couldn't help chuckling throaty and deep. "I'm not sick anymore, my husband," I murmured.

I seemed incapable of denying my urges, but the sound of a lock clicking made me shift my gaze to the door. We were no longer in the kitchen but in the privacy of our bedroom in our private tower of the castle.

"This little gift of teleportation comes in handy," I said with a laugh.

"You're not well, Susanna..." he murmured, his last protest before I drove him to the edge of reason and made love to him like an animal unleashed.

Only when we'd both reached temporary fulfillment did I bend over him, straddled beneath me, and lick his mouth. "I know you're a vampire, Nicholai. A *strigoii*. But how is it you eat food? How is it you seem so human?"

"Like all of my kind, I crave warmth. Food and fire provide that. All the fairytales and legends you have heard are not necessarily true, Susanna. Vampires are not evil. We are capable of great love, just as we are prone to loneliness. We require both the soil of our home to survive indefinitely, and the frequent contact with members of our clan. That is why my family rarely travels far from home, and my brother and sister come home often. It is why I had to leave you all those times, for endless months, even when I did not wish to."

"And why you wanted me to come here with you," I guessed. "Did you bite me? Did you make me one, too?"

A look of sheer agony crossed his face. "Oh my love, I could not. Not without your consent. And even then, I could not bear to give you this curse I have carried for centuries of loneliness so intense, I longed countless times to step out into the sun and end it once and for all."

"Like your sister Nadia?"

His surprise melted into acceptance, and he nodded, his eyes closed. "She chose the burning over another century of this curse. This loneliness."

"She didn't find love?"

"We are the only of our kind. God's chosen to control evil. We do not make others like us. We are not like the *vérfarkas*. This is why I tried so hard not to love you, Susanna. I just could not stay away from you. My heart refused to be turned from you."

"Your father is undead. That's why he's here, but he's not?"

"He sleeps for decades, as we all must. He, too, cannot bear eternity as an immortal with no end. Viktor, my sister and other brother and my mother seem to do this so easily."

"And now we're together, and we have a child on the way."

His anguish surprised me.

"I was afraid before, Nicholai, but now that I'm with you..."

He shook his head, his expression not changing. "I was not the one who bit you, my love. You were bitten by a werewolf. I suspected this long ago. I sensed the gene inside you, but only tested it recently, when we were in the States. Your genes match that of a werewolf. You must have been in contact with them once, long ago."

I knew then that the nightmare haunting me for most of my life—the one I hated to dream or even think about—was real. "I was scratched. I thought it was just a nightmare I had sometimes, when I couldn't prevent it. My parents never spoke of it afterward. We'd been a vacation…I don't know where, somewhere outside the States. My aunt Maggie was bitten, and a man told my parents she would become a werewolf. I suppose that's why she secluded herself far away from everyone she loved. I'd only been scratched, the man told my parents, and the gene was now in my bloodstream. The werewolves would hunt me. I would know them on instinct, and I'd lead an unfulfilled life until they called me and bit me. Maggie said she'd kept an eye on me from afar in all that time. She knew how afraid my parents were of me. Why didn't my parents just let me stay with her?"

"It would have been dangerous. Though your aunt is half-human and therefore can live some of the time normally, when the moon is full, she would shift and become a danger to you."

I swallowed the instinctive fear in my throat.

Nicholai nodded. "At the full moon this night, you will become one of them as you were always meant to, *szeretőm*."

I remembered his mother's words as if from a dream. *"Only your blood can save both your beloved and your child, Nicholai."*

"How can werewolves be real?"

"How can vampires? Werewolves are vile creatures, Susanna. They prey on the evil and the pure without distinction. They are cunning. Bloodthirsty. They fight constantly among themselves, and very often kill each other. They make more and more of their own kind, uncaring. Vampires are all that can stop them."

"'No cure, except that she be bitten by a vampire!'" I said out loud, remembering the old man's cackling words in my nightmare.

"Yes, only vampires can destroy werewolves."

"Silver bullets?"

He shook his head. "Silver bullets stop them only temporarily. They regenerate just as vampires do." He reached up to touch my throat, and I remembered how quickly my scratches had healed. "I should never have brought you here, Susanna, no matter how much I longed for my home. My own soil."

"What will happen to the baby if I become one of them?"

His eyes filled with pity. "What do your instincts tell you, my love? Wolves kill the offspring of non-alpha adults in packs. Does your heart not tell you they will kill our child because it is not of them? In all the centuries my family has lived, we know so little. We vampires have never conceived. We have never mated with mortals. Nor have we mated with the werewolves. I cannot know what might happen to our child, except that which I fear they will do if we let them."

"Will the change stop if you bite me? Will your vampire blood take over the werewolf blood inside my veins?" I asked.

He didn't speak, and I said frantically, "Your mother claimed..."

"Yes, but my mother has no way of knowing! My brother has spent centuries 'womanizing' the gypsy females. They appear to be immune to everything a vampire could pass on to them, immune to everything except our charms. A child has never been conceived in all his reckless couplings. My family was made vampires, though we do not remember our mortal lives, nor how our dark curse was given to us."

His last words were drowned out with a howl that so shattered the silence, I sat bolt upright. Werewolves, calling me. I heard them, felt them, sensed them inside me like an incurable need. They'd surrounded the walls. They would come for me if I didn't go out to them.

Out of nowhere, an answering howl erupted in my chest and ripped through the dead silence of the castle. I was horrified when it died away only to be followed with responding howls from without. It had been I who had growled like an animal that night in my loft, I realized. I knew it now, and I wondered how I'd spent so many years convincing myself I wasn't what I knew deep down I was meant to become.

"Choose, Susanna!" Nicholai urged harshly. "The moon is rising."

I couldn't comprehend my own hesitation. All my life, I'd been alone. I hadn't understood why I was so different from everyone else. A lone wolf, a creature of the night...one who desperately wanted to belong to my own pack. I knew where I belonged finally. But now there was Nicholai. I loved him and he loved me, despite his abhorrence to werewolves. I wanted to share my life and our child with him.

I looked down at my husband, and a hunger grew fiercely inside me. I could taste his blood again... *I* could infect *him*. But I accepted instantly that I could never hurt him.

"I belong with you, Nicholai. No matter what I am or what I become this night, I want to be with you for eternity."

I reached back and lifted my hair to expose my throat to him. Sudden pain grasped me, the excruciating sense that my body was again restructuring itself from the inside out.

Nicholai sat up and wrapped his arms around me as though realizing how I was coming apart. In agony and fear, I tilted my head back, not knowing whether I would live or die from this second bite. Whether I would become a werewolf even with Nicholai's *strigoii* blood. Whether our child would survive or be an abomination neither of us could endure. I knew only that I would love Nicholai no matter what happened.

Epilogue

Even vampires knew fear, I learned early on. Though I didn't become a werewolf the night Nicholai bit me, took my blood and I drank from him, I worried that the vampire blood wouldn't be strong enough to destroy the werewolf blood coursing through me.

I worried for our child, growing heavy and strong within me. I'd never borne a child, even as a human, but I was certain the one inside me wasn't normal in the human sense. He was too strong even in his protective home within my body. And I doubt many pregnant women craved both ice cream and endless amounts of blood. Even if our son—I felt sure of his sex—wasn't a combination between a vampire and a werewolf, even if he was only a vampire, or possibly a mortal, I had no idea what to expect. What did vampire babies eat? What did vampire mothers feed human babies? How in the world would Nicholai and I explain why Mommy and Daddy drank blood if he didn't? What if he was evil, as the werewolves were? Could we let him go to his own kind?

"Will he understand us? Will he feel like an alien?" I worried on the way down to dinner many months later.

"Our love for him won't allow that, Susanna. His life will be happy, such as it is. In whatever way it is."

That I wanted to believe. I didn't want to consider that our son would be so ungodly, we couldn't bear to look upon him.

That night, after Nicholai and I worshipped in the chapel, our son was born. He was nothing like I expected. Beautiful. A head full of thick, dark hair was his only werewolf legacy. Human in countenance and form. I laughed when I saw his tiny vampire teeth.

Worry took form in me again when he began rooting at my breasts hungrily. His expression as he settled in against me to nurse resembled one of pure contentment. I loved him fiercely in that instant.

"You're perfect, Tivadar, gift from God."

As though recognizing my voice as well as understanding my words, Tivadar opened his eyes. Not a hint of white surrounded the black pupil.

I smiled through tears and looked up at Nicholai beside us to exclaim, "Oh, look, he has your eyes, honey!"

You can find ALL our books on our website at:
http://www.writers-exchange.com

You can find ALL Karen's books at:
http://www.writers-exchange.com/Karen-Wiesner/

Romance:
http://www.writers-exchange.com/category/genres/romance/

JOIN ONE LIST. GET FIVE FREE BOOKS.

Sign up for Writers Exchange E-Publishing's newsletter and *immediately* get a free Novel! A new download link to a novel in each of our five main genres will hit your inbox once a week for the next four weeks!

http://bit.ly/WEE-Newsletter

You'll be kept up to date about our new releases and what we've been up to every month, including our blog highlights.

About the Author

Creating realistic, unforgettable characters one story at a time...

In addition to being a popular writing reference instructor and writer, professional blurbologist and freelance editor, Karen Wiesner is the accomplished author of 143 titles published in the past 22 years, which have been nominated/won 134 awards, with 21 more releases contracted for spanning many genres and formats. Karen's books cover such genres as women's fiction, romance, mystery/police procedural/cozy, suspense/thriller, paranormal/supernatural, futuristic, fantasy, science fiction, gothic, inspirational/Christian, thriller, horror, chick-lit, and action/adventure. She also writes children's books, poetry, and writing reference titles.

Visit Karen's website at http://www.karenwiesner.com. Check out her author page at Facebook here: http://www.facebook.com/KarenWiesnerAuthor.

If you enjoyed this author's book, then please place a review up at the site of purchase and any social media sites you frequent!

2-in-1 Inspirational Romance Novellas by Karen Wiesner

Publisher Book Page:
http://www.writers-exchange.com/2-in-1-inspirational-romance/

"The Amethyst Angel"

Elena Lopez's father has decided to play matchmaker with his long-time friend and neighbor, Marta Delgado, when Marta's nephew comes to town. Elena has a secret though: She's always loved Marta's own son Pablo. An amethyst angel belonging to a dying boy reminds Elena that spending her life waiting for something to happen isn't living and that love must be shared. Can she take the risk of telling Pablo her feelings even if he doesn't share her love?

"A Home for Christmas"

All Christie Renata Zondervon has ever wanted is a family, especially at Christmas-time. Craig Stevens has dried her tears, held her hand, listened to her talk about her hopes and fears at any time of day or night. She's never looked at him romantically before...until he invites her to spend Christmas with his family.

How does a painfully shy man reveal his heart without voicing the words that could lead to rejection? Craig has given himself twelve days to convince Christie he can be the man of her dreams. Now it's a countdown to win her heart or bust!

Cowboy Fever Series by Karen Wiesner
Contemporary Romance Anthology

Publisher Book Page:
http://www.writers-exchange.com/cowboy-fever-series/

Return to cowboy country in Fever, Texas, where the heat isn't the only thing causing a fever! See if you can find the heirloom wedding band in each story!

COWBOY FEVER SERIES

A compilation of the first five novellas in the series including:

Wings of Love, Book 1

When Wings Mackenzie falls in love, it's for life, and Amanda is the woman he has his heart set on. He struggles to get his business matters in hand so he can settle down with her. But when he returns home, ready to make the ultimate commitment to Amanda, he finds her long gone.

Losses and Gains, Book 2

Four years ago, Triple Aces Ranch co-owner, Lance Olsen, lost his wife and son in a fire. When her sister, his first love, comes home to Fever, sparks fly. But can an old flame be rekindled?

For Always, Book 3

As a young man, Jared had no idea how to share the intensity of his feelings with Alana. Instead, he'd awkwardly promised her he'd always be there for her. But she isn't looking for a bodyguard even when her up-on-coming politician husband begins taking the pressures of campaigning out on her. True to his promise, Jared runs to her rescue, but he open up and become the prince who'll love her for always?

Taming April, Book 4

Shawn Jacobs is the ultimate ladies' man. But when a former classmate of his shows up in treacherous high heels and designer clothing, asking him to train her father's horse, Shawn knows it isn't just the wild horse that needs to be tamed.

The Only One, Book 5

Five years ago, Ken and Karla were madly in love and expecting their first child. Tragedy drove them into opposite corners. When Ken shows up with her brothers at the exotic dance club she's been working as a waitress, she sees he hasn't changed. Can Ken prove she's still the only one for him?

DRIFTER'S HEART, Book 6

Easy to love, hard to hold... Maggie May's pa is still looking for the cowboy who knocked up his daughter. Just when Maggie thinks it'll never happen, the drifter she loves shows up, suddenly wise to the fact that his efforts to quiet her endless stream of conversation had ended with a child. This time, Maggie May plans to get him back in her clutches—and win his heart forever.

Kaleidoscope Series by Karen Wiesner
Contemporary Romance Anthology

Publisher Book Page:
http://www.writers-exchange.com/kaleidoscope-series/

Kaleidoscope Office Building provides employment to nine hot, young singles--all about to make a love connection. Working 9 to 5 has never been so complicated...or so much fun!

A compilation of all seven novellas in the series including:

Perfect Cadence, Book 1

While holed up at the family cabin mourning a lost loved one, the last thing Joshua Lewis expects to find is the drop-dead beautiful woman he'd regretted abandoning a decade earlier naked in his bed.

In Cahoots With Cupid, Book 2

Angela Lewis returns home to Fever, Texas for a wedding. Kiowa Mackenzie has every intention of tackling the bridesmaids to make sure Angela catches the bride's bouquet!

Behind Amethyst Eyes, Book 3

Amethyst-eyed, bespectacled Aimee Cooper has had a secret crush on muscle-bound accountant Rob Channing for years--even while one of her best friends dated him. When Aimee's father dies, she's left to mourn and sort out the complicated mess his estate has fallen into. In life's strange serendipity, this tragedy gives her an "in" to get close to the man of her dreams.

Jordana's Chair, Book 4

Dex has been intrigued by his neighbor since she moved into his building a year ago--though, or perhaps *because*--she's nothing like the glamour girls he's used to. Jordana barely speaks English, has worn the same two outfits since he's known her, and her living space is empty. No one he's ever known could display such joy over a new chair. Is this ladies' man officially off the market?

Paper Tiger, Book 5

Roni has a secret past she doesn't want to look back and confront, but can she risk losing the man she loves because of what could be a true threat...or merely a paper tiger?

Cabin Fever, Book 6

When single mother Shayna's son Ty begins to exhibit an inability to cope with the lack of a father-figure in his life, his elementary school teacher reaches out to Shayna. Can hunky widower Dakota Loring to prove he's the real deal?

The Longest Night, Book 7

After three short years of a marriage spent mostly apart, Jolie has decided to get the child she wants and forget the naive illusion of marital bliss. During one endless night, Jag tries to convince her he's in their relationship for the long haul while she tries to distract him with every sweet seduction in the book.